Happily

Ever After

Elizabeth Maxwell

A TOUCHSTONE BOOK
Published by Simon & Schuster
New York   London   Toronto   Sydney   New Delhi

Touchstone
A Division of Simon & Schuster, Inc.
1230 Avenue of the Americas
New York, NY 10020

This book is a work of fiction. Any references to historical events, real people, or real places are used fictitiously. Other names, characters, places, and events are products of the author's imagination, and any resemblance to actual events or places or persons, living or dead, is entirely coincidental.

First Touchstone trade paperback edition March 2014

TOUCHSTONE and colophon are registered trademarks of Simon & Schuster, Inc.

For information about special discounts for bulk purchases, please contact Simon & Schuster Special Sales at 1-866-506-1949 or business@simonandschuster.com.

The Simon & Schuster Speakers Bureau can bring authors to your live event. For more information or to book an event contact the Simon & Schuster Speakers Bureau at 1-866-248-3049 or visit our website at www.simonspeakers.com.

Designed by Aline C. Pace

Manufactured in the United States of America

10 9 8 7 6 5 4 3 2 1

Library of Congress Cataloging-in-Publication Data

Maxwell, Elizabeth, 1969– Happily Ever After / Elizabeth Maxwell.

pages cm

1. Divorced women—Fiction. 2. Women novelists—Fiction. 3.

Self-realization in women—Fiction. I. Title.

PS3613.C585455H37 2014

813'.6—dc23

2013017339

ISBN 978-1-4767-3266-4
ISBN 978-1-4767-3267-1 (ebook)

For my parents, Henry and Eva Von Ancken

midlife crisis

noun

a period of emotional turmoil in middle age character-
ized especially by a strong desire for change

(Merriam-Webster's Collegiate Dictionary, Eleventh Edition)

Happily

Ever After

Chapter 1

Stolen Secrets,
Chapter One

At exactly 8:45, Lily Dell pushed through the rotating doors of New York's Jensen & Richardson Communications and smiled at the security guard. She was running late, but that was no reason to be unfriendly.

"How are you today, Hank?" she asked.

The older man tipped his cap to her. "Fine, Miss Dell. Thanks for asking."

"Have a good day, okay?"

"As long as the sun is shining and I have air to breathe," he said with a wink.

Lily had the same exchange with Hank every morning, but that was okay. Lily found routines comforting. On some level, she knew it was because of her childhood, but there was no point in digging into that muck. She'd escaped it. That was enough for her.

"Wait!" Lily called as she ran for the elevator banks. Her office was on the fifty-eighth floor, and it could take forever for an elevator to show up at ground level during the morning rush. A bleached-blond woman with long pink fingernails stuck an arm between the elevator doors, holding them while Lily squeezed in.

"Thank you," Lily whispered to the woman.

The elevator moved in fits and starts, stopping repeatedly until it reached the thirtieth floor, when Lily finally found herself alone. Quickly, she dug into her handbag for a lipstick. At the rate she was moving, there was no way she was going to have time for a pit stop in the ladies' room to fix her makeup before meeting Mr. Hathaway.

Fumbling to open the lipstick without dropping her suit jacket, laptop case, or black leather purse, Lily lost her grip on the sleek tube and sent it tumbling down her crisp white shirt, leaving a trail of blushing peach as it went.

"Shit!" she cried.

"Oh, it's not so bad as all that," came a voice, and from the shadows of the seemingly empty elevator stepped a man. He was tall and lean, with jet-black hair and unreadable eyes the color of moss. His skin was pale and stood out against the dark pinstripe of his expensive suit. She

noticed the edge of a faint scar to the side of his right eyebrow. He smiled at her, showing off just a hint of his perfect teeth.

She tried to smile back, but suddenly the elevator was much too small.

"We've met," he said quietly, taking a step toward her. "Do you remember?"

What a question! She'd spent every waking moment since the reception last week trying to figure out who the beautiful man was but to no avail. It was the Keller Champagne marketing launch party, and although Lily hated to admit it, she'd had a few too many samples of the product. She'd been making her way toward the restrooms when this man, who now stood in the elevator with her, appeared.

Over a few yards of empty space, their eyes met, and time slowed and stretched as Lily suddenly became aware of every molecule in her body being pulled toward this stranger. They didn't stop walking. They glided by one another, their eyes locked.

"Good evening," the man said.

"Yes," Lily croaked.

"You look lovely," he said.

Before she could say thank you or ask his name or beg him to explain *what* had just happened, he gave her a mock salute and disappeared around the corner. It took almost a full minute for Lily to regain her bearings and chase after him. But by the time she reached the reception hall, he was nowhere to be seen.

"I do remember," Lily said now. Her voice sounded strange, as if it were coming from outside of her.

Slowly, the man bent down to retrieve her lipstick from the floor of the elevator. His motions were deliberate and smooth; she could see his broad shoulders straining against the fabric of his suit.

"You dropped this," he said, holding the tube out to Lily. His hands were big and graceful, not two qualities that normally went together in her limited experience. As she reached for the lipstick, their eyes met and the temperature in the elevator soared. A hot flush rose on Lily's cheeks, far brighter than the lipstick that now stained the front of her shirt.

"Thank . . . thank you," she stammered. When she took the lipstick, her fingers brushed the man's cool skin and the cuff of his suit jacket. The signal from her fingertips raced immediately up her arm and down through her stomach, coming firmly to rest between her thighs. She shuddered despite the rising heat. A wave of unfamiliar lust washed over her, rendering her momentarily dizzy. Lily never reacted to men this way. She was measured, careful, logical. She'd learned her lesson about what happened when you weren't. But her body did not seem to care.

"Oh," Lily murmured, squeezing her thighs together. It felt good. The man took a step closer. He gave off a

warm, citrusy scent that did not help her dizziness. His smile was gone. He eyed her as if she were prey, a great eagle about to dive on a helpless field mouse. Her legs threatened to buckle in high heels that no longer felt even remotely stable.

"Your shirt," he whispered. Lily was sure he could see her heart pounding through the thin fabric of her clothing. Did he feel this too?

"I think it's ruined," he said. He was so close now she could see the flawless surface of his skin. She could think of nothing but how badly she wanted him to touch her. Anywhere.

With agonizing slowness, he ran a finger down her cheek and into the hollow of her throat. There, he applied the slightest bit of pressure, making her gasp. Her body, as if detached from her brain, arched toward him.

Please, she thought. I can't do this.

His finger continued to travel down over her collarbone, easily pushing aside her shirt and slipping between the lacy edge of her bra and her skin. She forced herself to hold his eyes, which showed only focus. Lifting the fabric of her bra, he made room for the rest of his hand to slide around the outside of her breast.

Scream, she told herself. Call for help. But the only sound she seemed capable of making was another desperate "oh."

With a sudden forceful motion, the man pulled her

shirt and her bra strap off her shoulder to reveal her full breast. It looked white and strange in the dim lights of the elevator, at odds with the rest of her skin. He cupped her gently in one hand, bent down and ran his tongue over her hard exposed nipple, taking it between his teeth and gently tugging. Bolts of electricity shot through Lily, and she wanted to howl, to beg for more. Instead, she bit her lip and grabbed the wall for support, sure she was about to faint. The very lonely place between her legs throbbed in anticipation. How long had it been? Forever.

"You taste so ... sweet," the man whispered.

How much time did they have? Was it enough? She could not believe she was having these thoughts! Who was this man making her body quiver like jelly? As if reading her mind, he brought his lips to her ear.

"Fast," he said, sliding one of those big hands between her knees and moving it up along the freshly shaved, smooth skin of her inner thighs. Pants would have saved her here, whereas a skirt spelled certain doom. His hand reached her ordinary cotton panties, already soaked, and for a flash she wished she'd worn something more special, something with lace. As he pressed his fingers against her, she sucked in a breath of air.

Leaning in close so she was forced to look into his eyes, he ripped back her panties and ran his smooth fingers across...

"Mom!"

Huh? Oh, Allison. Damn.

"What is it, honey?" I call. A trickle of sweat runs down my back. Is my office hot?

"Come. Here."

"Okay, Ali. I'm coming."

It's 11:15 on a Thursday night, and I know two things. The first is that Lily Dell was about to have sex in an elevator where time has no meaning, cotton rips like wet paper towels, and moaning is sexy rather than a sign of mental illness. The second is that my own chances of having sex tonight in an elevator, or anywhere for that matter, are exactly zero. And sadly, those are odds you can bet your life on.

Chapter 2

didn't plan for it to go this way. No one fantasizes about being a slightly overweight, middle-aged, divorced mother desperately in need of an eyebrow wax and some sort of Pilates intervention. No one dreams of driving a blue Toyota minivan with unidentifiable food particles wedged between the seats or owning a sofa with coffee ring stains on the arms. But these things happen regardless. And then you must live with them.

My name is Sadie Fuller. Sometimes when I look in the mirror, I see my twenty-five-year-old self. She's young and fresh and ready for anything life decides to throw at her. Other times, I walk past a storefront and catch a glimpse of myself now, at forty-six, and I wonder who on earth it could be staring back at me. Surely that woman with the crow's-feet and the laugh lines and the sun damage isn't me. That woman must be my mother.

In addition to the minivan and the coffee ring stains, I have an eleven-year-old daughter named Allison, a dog named Perkins, and an ex-husband who is really very lovely except for the fact that he's gay and I'm a woman.

I have brown hair that used to be glossy but is now chemically treated, and brown eyes that don't work quite as well as they once did. I stash reading glasses like I used to stash cigarettes. Never know when an emergency might arise. I give regularly to Planned Parenthood and the Democratic National Committee, and for some reason, this year, I raised my hand to help manage the annual school fund-raiser. Being as I already pay forty-five thousand dollars a year for Allison to attend fifth grade at the prestigious Holt Hall, I kind of thought that might be it as far as parent involvement went. My premise was obviously a false one.

Which just reinforces what we already know—assumptions will get you nowhere. For example, you might look at me and think, stay-at-home mom who has let herself go, and never realize that at night, while the rest of suburbia sleeps, I write erotic romances under the name K. T. Briggs.

Perhaps you've heard of me, if sex in elevators or on conference tables or in airplane lavatories is your thing? Attorneys think about briefs, doctors think about test results, I think about beautiful people fornicating in inappropriate places.

When asked what kinds of books I write, I say romance. It's not like I'm a prostitute or anything, but I worry that in the eyes of my affluent, conservative neighbors, there might not be much difference. Smut is smut. No one wants to discuss how best to

describe oral sex during the cookies and coffee portion of our monthly PTA meetings. We're *moms*, for God's sake! We're here to talk about the nutritional value of the average sandwich and whether or not it's appropriate to take third graders to see *Wicked* on Broadway. Who has *time* to think about sex in a sun-drenched rose garden with George Clooney, or Channing Tatum, if you like them a little bit younger?

However, I would not be able to pay the mortgage, tuition, car insurance, or alimony if not for a whole lot of moms out there whiling away their free time fantasizing about fucking just about anywhere but in their own beds. And I'm grateful to each and every one of them.

I stumble down the hallway toward Allison's voice. She sits up in bed, a blanket draped over her shoulders, squinting as I flick on the light. Her face, the spitting image of her father's, is flushed.

"What's up?" I ask, sinking down next to her. Pushing a lock of dirty blond hair aside, I instinctively run the back of my hand across her forehead. It's cool to the touch. A few freckles dot her nose and cheeks.

"Bad dream," she says, leaning into me. My eleven-year-old is right on the cusp of becoming a full-fledged teenager and thus being required to hate me until she turns twenty. So for now, I take care to cherish the moments when she allows me to wrap my arms around her. I figure if I store up enough of them, they might see me through the dry years ahead.

"What was the dream about?" I ask.

"Fuzzy things with fangs," Allison says, snuggling closer. She smells like mountain air in the summer, fresh and soapy, and I'm struck, as I often am, by her potential. She can be anything. How amazing to have that, even if you're too young to understand what it means.

"And?" I ask. I refrain from suggesting she read something without vampires for once because that will make her pull away and she feels very good in my arms right now.

"They were chasing me and Perkins," she continues.

At the sound of her name, Perkins, a thirty-one-flavors mutt, raises her head off the bed. She would surely lay down her life to protect us, but being as she is the size of a loaf of bread, it might not have much impact. After a stretch and a toothy yawn, Perkins goes back to sleep. She will stay here all night, faithfully guarding Allison's feet, no matter how many times she gets kicked in the head for her efforts.

"Where were they chasing you?" I ask.

"I don't know. Places." Allison's eyelids flutter. I pat her pillow, and she dutifully lays her head back on it. She smiles at me. I know what comes next.

"Will you stay?" she asks. Her voice is sweet, like she chugged a pitcher of pixie dust, but I fall for it every time. Mostly because I want to.

"Yes," I say. "Only a few minutes. I'm working."

"On the new story?"

Yes. My publisher says there has to be a *story* in there somewhere. It can't all be sex, because that would make it plain old

pornography. Erotica has substance. It has a plot. It has . . . whatever. I know. No one watches porn for the acting, and no one reads erotica for the plot.

But this is something my eleven-year-old does not need to hear quite yet. I lie down next to her, wrap my arms tighter around her long, lean body, and manage the light switch with my toe. This makes Allison giggle.

"Go to sleep," I whisper. "It's late. School tomorrow."

I watch as her eyes close and her red lips fall open with the rhythmic mouth breathing of sleep. If I could, I would freeze everything right at this moment. I would hold on to my beautiful child forever, never leaving this room, never changing a thing.

But time is short and I have pages to go before I sleep. I untangle myself from Allison and tiptoe back to my office. I take a few sips of red wine. Now where was I? Elevator sex. Right.

Leaning in close so Lily was forced to look into his eyes, he ripped back her panties and ran his smooth fingers across her hot, throbbing folds of skin. Oh, such exquisite pain and pleasure side by side. It was all Lily could do not to tear off the rest of her clothes and wrap her naked body around him, begging him to take her here against the elevator wall.

A chiming cell phone interrupts my elevator sex. Am I to be deprived of a climax yet again? Tonight may not be my night. I'm as unlucky as a fourteen-year-old boy at Catholic school.

Of course, it's my ex-husband, Roger, calling. We speak every day. Or, more accurately, Roger speaks and I listen. I have written entire chapters with him chatting away on the phone. He would be crushed if he knew how effectively I can tune him out. I prop my feet up on my desk and answer.

"Roger."

"Sadie."

"It's late, Roger."

"But I have a problem and it just *cannot* wait," he says. All of Roger's problems are urgent.

"What is it?" I ask.

"I don't think I can marry Fred," he whispers.

"Were you planning on marrying Fred?"

"We talked about it yesterday, but then I meditated on it and I think the answer has to be no."

"Did Fred ask you to marry him? Directly?"

"Well, not exactly."

"Is Fred there right now?"

"Yes. In bed."

With a vision of Roger huddled on his toilet with the bathroom door closed whispering into his cell phone, I tip back toward my laptop. I scan the open page. Where was I?

"Sadie, are you listening to me?"

"Of course, Roger."

"Did you mail my check?"

"Of course, Roger."

"Good," he says. "Things are a little tight this month. The studio doesn't do so well in the spring. People want to be *outside*. I have no idea what that is about."

According to Roger, people don't like to do yoga in the winter because it's too cold or in the summer because it's too hot or in the autumn because they can go outside and look at the pretty fall foliage in Central Park. So every month is a little tight for Roger. I was hoping Fred might stick. Fred is rich. But apparently, Roger meditated himself right out of that idea.

"I don't know either," I say. I add a sentence to my manuscript. Reread it. Delete it. I take another swig of my wine.

"How's my baby girl?" Roger asks.

"Sleeping. It's night, remember?"

"Right."

"Hey, what's the coolest bar in New York right now?" I ask.

"Buddha, on Twenty-Third," Roger answers without pause.

"Straight?"

"Not even a little."

"I need to put my hero in a trendy New York bar," I say. "But I think it has to be a straight bar for this book."

"What about the hot dog and popcorn counter in Target?" Roger says with a laugh.

"Not funny."

"Sorry."

"Is there anything else, Roger? I'm at forty-two hundred words and I'd really like to hit fifty-five hundred and go to bed."

"Sorry, Sadie," he says. "It's just I'm so *lonely* now that I've decided to end this thing with Fred. What if I never find another man?"

"You've never even had lunch alone," I remind him, which is almost true. If Roger dumps Fred tomorrow, he will be madly in love again by Sunday brunch. Roger does not waste time mulling over why a relationship failed. Damn the torpedoes, full speed ahead! I grudgingly respect him for it because I know a lot about never finding another man.

"I miss you, Sadie," he says.

"No, you don't," I say.

"You know what I mean."

"I do. Good night, Roger."

I hang up on him before he can trap me into a full dissection of his romantic troubles.

I married Roger for one reason: he was the father of the child neither of us meant to conceive. As I had given up on kids and romance and had accepted my spinsterhood, this came as a bit of a surprise. We were not an ideal couple. Roger had no ambition. He was needy. And I was the scarred veteran of a spectacularly failed romance, suspicious of all things male. I liked Roger well enough, but I did not love him in the heart-pounding, pulse-racing way I had always associated with marriage. Plus, the sex wasn't great, but I dismissed that as being unimportant. Obviously the idea of a baby had overwhelmed all reason, and we quickly convinced ourselves we were a perfect fit.

"Let's get married!"

"Let's be a family!"

It wasn't a hard sell really. Roger was nice. He held doors

and pulled out chairs. He loved romantic comedies, no matter how poorly miscast. He loved to cook and entertain. And most important, he was over the moon about being a dad.

"I never saw this happening for me," he said, his head resting on my swelling belly. In retrospect, I should have asked him to explain the "why" behind that statement in detail, but I was blissed out with pregnancy hormones and not thinking clearly.

I divorced Roger because he fell in love with a man named James. Roger said all the yoga had helped him evolve to his authentic self, and his authentic self turned out to be gay. Over an expensive dinner, paid for by me, he walked me through the steps of this evolution. I did not want to go on this particular walk. I kept reminding him we had a child together, as if that were somehow going to change his sexual orientation. At the end of the meal, Roger gave me a sad smile and asked for a divorce. His heart needed to chase James. And then Tim, followed by Andre and Seymour and Jacob and Ian and Oliver and Gavin and so on and so forth.

After my safe harbor of Roger turned out to be in shark-infested waters, I decided, quite reasonably, I had played all the angles, tried all the variations, and I was done. I was giving up men, romance, and anything related to either. The new, practical, very alone me would be just fine.

Of course, it only took about six months to realize I would never actually be alone again. In that short span, Roger's evolution took a hairpin turn and he began to behave like an insecure teenager. I now had two children to mind. It was a sobering thought for a newly single mother.

The wall clock indicates it's close to midnight, and I quit at midnight no matter where I am or what I've accomplished. Allison will be up asking for things by 7:00 A.M., and if I don't log at least six hours in the sack, I'm done for. The only advantage of sleeping alone is that you know you're going to sleep. I mean, what the hell else are you going to do?

Now where was I?

But before Lily could even get her mind around what was happening, this intense and fiery man returned all her garments to exactly how they'd been. No. No. No!

"It's really too bad about the shirt," he said, stepping away from her.

Lily, still leaning on the wall, felt her whole body quiver. She was nothing more than a shell, now filled with lust and longing. Unable to even open her mouth, she clutched her laptop bag to her chest, as if she could simply disappear behind it forever. Her breath came in ragged gasps.

Calm down, she told herself.

The elevator chose that moment to land smoothly on the fifty-eighth floor. The doors slid back to reveal a modern reception area and Peter Jensen himself standing by the large and not altogether welcoming receptionist's desk.

"Lily, great," Jensen said with a grin. "I see you've already had a chance to meet Aidan Hathaway."

Lily turned to the man whose intense eyes now registered a degree of amusement.

"You're Hathaway?" she asked, her legs almost too wobbly to carry her out of the elevator with any dignity.

In response, Aidan Hathaway gave her a smile that could only mean trouble.

Chapter 3

At 6:50 on Friday morning, Allison stands at the foot of my bed and clears her throat. In the background, the air conditioner hums. It's only April, but we are on day two of a heat wave that is making the local meteorologists hysterical. They keep throwing out words like *Armageddon* and *Apocalypse.* Yes, it's hot, really fucking hot, in fact, but I don't exactly see the end of the world angle, at least not this morning.

"Mom? Are you awake?"

"No," I mutter, pulling the blankets up over my head. "I'm not even close."

"Which jeans?" Allison yanks my covers back and shoves two pairs of dark blue, impossibly small pants in my face. How can a body be that rail thin and still house all the necessary internal organs? Maybe it's the macrobiotic brown rice her father feeds her. He swears it will change my life. I tell him so will macaroni and cheese, although I doubt we're talking about the same kind of change.

"Mom, wake up! Which jeans?"

"They're the same," I say.

"No," my daughter says emphatically. "They are *not* the same. You aren't paying attention."

"You're right," I say. "I'm sleeping."

This earns me a classic tweener pout. Allison's lower lip juts out far enough to provide a comfy landing spot for the finches I hear outside my window. But I know better than to mention it. A pout I can handle. A full-on snit will have to wait until after I've had coffee.

"Those," I say, pointing to the pair of jeans in her left hand.

"I don't like those."

"Okay, the other ones."

"Thanks, Mom," Allison says, and skips off to her room, where I'm sure she will commence agonizing about what shirt to wear. If I get up now, I can be safely locked in the bathroom by the time she comes back.

Downstairs I hear the door slam, which means it's now exactly 7:00 A.M. You know those atomic clocks that are so accurate they lose only one second every 30 million years? Well, they've got nothing on Greta. My German housekeeper, somewhere between the ages of sixty and infinity, walks in the door every morning at exactly seven o'clock. In the ten years we've been together, she has never once been late, making it the longest and most fulfilling

relationship I've had in my adult life. I mean, Greta *does* things. She cooks. She folds. She irons. If she's mad, she refuses to acknowledge my existence for a few hours and then gets over it. There's no backstabbing or cheating. I trust her completely. That she may be the only person I can say that about is alarming only if I spend time thinking about it.

Plus, on the first day Greta and Allison met, when Allison was a mere twelve months old, they gazed into one another's eyes and fell in love. They simply adore each other. Sometimes when I watch them together, I feel as if I'm on the outside looking in, like I'm in a bubble with impenetrable walls.

One minute after the door slams, I hear dishes being hauled from the washer and put away. Next, the strong aroma of coffee wafts up the stairs and lures me from my bed. Downstairs, Greta hands me a mug with a layer of warm, foamy milk on the top. I want to kiss her, but she doesn't do touchy-feely with me. At all. Ever.

"Thank you and good morning," I say. She nods without saying a word and turns to Allison, who has joined us in the kitchen. Allison holds up two shirts.

"Which one?" she demands. I should have done the bathroom thing.

"Pancakes or waffles?" Greta shoots back.

"Pancakes," Allison says.

"The stripes," Greta says, pointing at a shirt. I watch this exchange like I'm a referee at the U.S. Open.

"Great!" I say. "That's all settled." Neither one acknowledges my existence. I take my coffee to the table and hide behind the pages of the local newspaper.

I don't do a lot of cooking. Allison says the food I prepare is awful because I don't pay attention and usually forget a key ingredient or two. Which is true. It can be distracting trying to figure out how many ways Aidan Hathaway and Lily Dell can fuck in 250 pages. It's not world peace, I know, but it does require concentration.

While Allison and Greta chatter in German, I, who did not grow up with a German housekeeper and speak little more of the language than *Ich bin ein Berliner,* stare blankly at the headlines and try to chart a course through the day that will allow for everyone's needs to be met. It won't work. Something will slip through the cracks. I've come to think of my to-do list as a work in perpetual progress. It is an epic that will span many years. It will never end! If I could make it more interesting, I might be able to convince my publisher to serialize it in an e-book.

"Do either of you need anything from Target?" I ask.

"Pink nail polish!" shouts Allison.

"Laundry detergent," says Greta.

Greta does most of our shopping, or "marketing" as she calls it. But she draws the line at Target and Home Depot. There is something about the vastness of these stores, the overwhelming quantities of cheap merchandise, that offends her sensibilities, and I understand this to be a nonnegotiable aspect of our relationship.

As I'm just about to clarify the shade of the pink and the

brand of the detergent, I'm suddenly swallowed whole by a prickly, cold sensation, as if the icy ghost of Christmas Future has wrapped himself around me and begun to squeeze.

Panic. I lean both hands on the marble kitchen island for balance, closing my eyes against the dizziness. A sheen of sweat breaks out across my forehead, and I shudder from its chill. I gasp, a sharp, awful sound. My lungs feel small and useless.

"Mom?"

I open my eyes to see Allison staring at me, alarm splashed all over her pretty face.

"Are you okay, Sadie?" Greta asks, simultaneously looking at me and flipping a pancake into the air, just to have it land perfectly dead center of the pan.

Slowly the tightness in my chest recedes. This is not my first panic attack. This is panic attack number 342. Or something like that. We are practically old friends. I gulp the rich, sweet-smelling air while trying not to look insane.

"I'm fine," I say, still clutching the counter. "Just a dizzy spell. Probably the heat."

I smile. I down a slice of toast and sip my coffee. Usually as a panic episode recedes I feel nothing but relief and genuine gratitude that it is not my permanent state. And yet right now I feel exceedingly unusual, like a part of me has split off and gone elsewhere, as if I might be floating. Greta turns back to the pancakes, but Allison keeps watching me, brows furrowed. I kiss her head.

"I'm fine," I say. "Eat your breakfast. We have to go to school."

I excuse myself to take a shower, but I don't head for the bathroom. Instead, I'm drawn toward my office, although I cannot explain why. My heart beats erratically, the detached feeling following in my wake. I want to take a shower and get dressed and take Allison to school. I don't want to go to my office. But what I want does not seem to matter.

I stand outside the closed door, pure panic rising in my throat at the prospect of opening it.

"Stop it, Sadie," I whisper. "Get a grip."

I place a hand on the doorknob. My teeth chatter. Sweat soaks the back of the gray T-shirt I wore to bed last night. The doctor said panic attacks were not uncommon in women my age and could come at any time, without warning.

"Sometimes they have triggers and sometimes they don't," she said with a distracted smile. She then proceeded to tell me a story about a woman roughly my age who was terrified every time she had to open the trunk of her car.

"She's sure she'll find a peacock in there," the doctor said.

A peacock? The doc nodded grimly. This was her way of telling me it could be worse. At least I wasn't afraid of peacocks in the trunk. But in some ways, a peacock was better than free-form panic. At least then, I would know to avoid car trunks. The doctor prescribed Xanax and told me to come back in two weeks.

I now carry the Xanax in my purse everywhere I go, like a talisman against the panic monster. I drink wine, telling myself it will calm my mind, which it does for a moment in time. But

these solutions are Band-Aids, and I wonder what will happen when they fall off.

Still standing outside my office, I count backward from ten and push open the door. It's empty. No peacocks. I sit down at my desk with a thud and run my fingers along its edge. I love this desk, its modern lines and no-nonsense approach. It's all business, and when I sit at it, so am I.

I start to relax, ready to begin the process of convincing myself that everything is perfectly fine. My laptop sits open on the desk, just as I left it last night. Up on the screen is the manuscript for *Stolen Secrets,* featuring Aidan Hathaway and Lily Dell. I focus on the blinking cursor, midway down the page, rhythmic and soothing. My eyes drift to the word count at the bottom of the screen. Sixty-two hundred words.

Impossible. I look away. I look back. I still see a sixty-two hundred word count. But ask any writer: word counts are not things we forget. They are a measure of progress, about the only one we get until we share the manuscript with an editor or a friend coached not to criticize a first draft too harshly. As well as I know that my nose is slightly crooked, I know I quit well shy of my fifty-five-hundred-word goal, at forty-two hundred to be exact. In fact, as I climbed into bed, I swore I'd make up the difference tonight. So where did the extra fifteen hundred words come from? A veil of dread covers me like a burka. Memory loss at forty-six years old? Early onset Alzheimer's? What happens to Allison and Greta and Perkins then? Before I can return to full hyperventilation, I hear a shout from downstairs.

"Mom, school! Aren't you out of the shower yet?"

How long have I been sitting here staring at my laptop? I reach up and feel my hair, bedraggled as usual. Nope. Never got to the shower, and now I've lost the chance. I will go through my morning looking like I just rolled out of bed because, technically, that will be true.

"We're going to be late, Mom. And it's *not* going to be my fault."

I jump out of the chair, and as I head for my room, I shed the plaid pajama pants and gray T-shirt only a single lady determined to stay that way would wear to bed, both now damp with the sweat of panic.

Chapter 4

Stolen Secrets

Chapter Two

Sitting at the bar in Gramercy Tavern, Lily tried to keep a blush of pure humiliation and anger from her cheeks. Just that very morning, after the elevator incident, Hathaway's secretary had called, requesting her presence tonight at seven o'clock.

"Give the maître d' your name and he will seat you in the correct position," the secretary said in a clipped British accent. "And don't be late. Mr. Hathaway doesn't like late."

Correct position? But the secretary was gone before Lily had a chance to clarify what exactly that meant.

"I'm not going," she announced to the three high walls of her cubicle. "No way." But here she was, because in the end, the anxious, slightly desperate feeling Aidan Hathaway produced in the pit of her stomach was impossible to ignore.

The maître d' took her name and sat her on a particular barstool.

"He likes his girls to face to the south," the man said, turning her slightly. "That way he can see you when he comes in but you can't see him." The maître d' relayed this information as if it were all quite ordinary. Not knowing what else to do, she thanked him and took her seat at the bar, the flush of anger making her glow.

After a moment, Lily turned so she faced the door of the bar. She would not play Hathaway's games.

Over the course of the day, Lily had convinced herself the only reason she was showing up was to clarify with Hathaway what, exactly, had happened in the elevator. Lily was not that kind of girl, and she felt this was something she had to make very clear. She was on a mission to restore her good name. A drink materialized in front of her. The bartender, a cute blond guy, gave her a wink.

"Pretty lady like you shouldn't be sitting here alone staring at the door," he said with a warm smile. "Whoever he is, if he can't show up on time, forget about him."

"Thank you," Lily said, raising the glass to her lips. The drink was pale purple and smelled of violets. "This is wonderful. What is it?"

"What's your name?" the bartender asked.

"Lily."

"Well, then that's what the drink is called. The Lily."

Lily cast her eyes down, a warm glow replacing the fiery anger of moments before. She didn't know if it was the alcohol or the flirtation.

"That's really sweet of you," she said, taking another sip.

Suddenly, the bartender's face fell. He grabbed a towel and began mopping quick circles on the bar even though it was so clean Lily could see her reflection.

"Excuse me," he said, and scurried away.

At that exact moment, a cold hand closed around Lily's neck. She gasped. Aidan Hathaway.

"Again, you look lovely, Lily," he said, keeping a light grip on the back of her neck. There was something about the way he said her name that made the bottom of her stomach drop. It was the sensation of longing. She wanted to be naked with him, tangled in his limbs and a mess of soft white sheets.

But she reminded herself she barely liked the guy. What sort of person has his secretary arrange for dates anyway? Couldn't he have called her? After all, she worked for his company. It wasn't like he couldn't get her phone number.

"I'm sorry I kept you waiting," he continued, pulling up the stool next to hers so their knees touched. "Work. I have something for you."

He handed her a shopping bag from Bloomingdale's. Inside was a wrapped box.

"Open it," he said.

Doing as she was told, she pulled out the box and stripped off the copper-colored wrapping paper, letting it fall to the floor. Gently, she loosened the box lid to reveal several layers of tissue paper. Her hands shook as she peeled back the tissue to reveal her shirt, the one she'd ruined with lipstick just earlier today. Unlike her shirt, this was not a knockoff; it was the real thing. Lily looked up at Hathaway, into his green eyes. All traces of anger evaporated.

"I don't know what to say," she said. "Thank you."

"It looked good on you," Aidan said. "It would be a shame not to have it anymore."

Oh, how she wanted him! It almost seemed too big to manage. And not at all logical. Everyone knew you did not sleep with the boss unless you wanted to derail your career. But this was Aidan Hathaway, New York City's most eligible bachelor.

Stick to your plan, Lily, she chided herself. Your mission.

Aidan didn't say anything. He just studied her face, a shadow clouding his eyes, as if he could read her thoughts.

"You're incredibly beautiful," he said slowly, his voice husky with emotion. "And you have no idea."

Don't say those things, Lily thought.

"Mr. Hathaway," she began. The speech was all prepared, rehearsed in front of the bathroom mirror in fact. Now she just had to deliver it. "I'm so honored to be lead

creative on the Hathaway account that I think it's important we maintain a professional relationship. I don't want any distractions. I want my full focus to be on marketing the many Hathaway brands to the world."

She felt the heat rise on her face, all the while held captive by his eyes. He smiled as she went on.

"Furthermore, I think I should explain that my, our, behavior in the elevator was, um, really . . ."

She sputtered, losing the words she'd so carefully assembled. She wished he would stop looking at her.

"Do go on," Aidan said, placing a hand casually on her thigh. She could smell him, the same warm citrusy scent that had made the elevator so small. It very effectively canceled out all other thought. He was inches from her.

"Are you done?" he asked.

Lily nodded. She could think of nothing but his hand on her thigh. The tips of his fingers grazed the hem of the very professional orange sheath dress she had changed into earlier. She gulped.

"Good," he said.

Before she knew it, he had swept her off her barstool and into his arms. His warm lips found hers, and he kissed her, long and hard and deep. His touch set off fireworks behind her eyelids. She wrapped her arms around his neck and held on. Suddenly, he pulled back and put those lush lips to her ear.

"I want you," he whispered. "I've wanted you from the moment I saw you. It's almost more than I can stand."

He slid a hand between her legs, far enough up that she forgot what she was thinking about.

"Do you want to come home with me?" he asked.

Again, Lily found her voice betrayed her. She nodded her head. Yes. Please.

"I want to possess you," he whispered. "To consume you."

There was something about the word *consume* that sent a cold shiver down her spine. Aidan Hathaway had a reputation for consuming anything and everything that caught his fancy. Yes, after the elevator, she'd done her research about the man himself, read all the gossip about his womanizing ways, how he was hot and heavy with a Brazilian model one day and on to a British rock star the next. She'd read about how he zeroed in on companies he wanted to acquire with an eaglelike precision and would not rest until they were neatly tucked away under the Hathaway Enterprises umbrella. He was intense on the basketball court, routinely getting out on the floor with the professional athletes whose teams he owned.

And when it came to philanthropy he was just as focused. Instead of giving over a pile of money and calling it a day, he went along to Africa or Asia or wherever to make sure the dollars he gave were spent appropriately.

He was known to fund entire ventures while on the road, if something caught his eye and seemed worthy.

Aidan Hathaway was twenty-nine years old.

His eyes held her, although she craved release. He seemed to see right into her soul, all the way down to the dirty, hidden stuff, the secrets she had never told anyone. She found herself wishing Hathaway Enterprises had never hired Jensen & Richardson Communications. But it was too late for that.

"Do you want what I want?" Aidan asked.

"Yes," she breathed, not even thinking about her answer. It came out like a sigh of relief.

His hand moved to the back of her dress. It was a beautiful Prada knockoff with a row of simple buttons up the back. She could feel his fingers pop a button and slide between the fabric and her skin. She shuddered. A part of her screamed out for him to stop, they were in a public place for God's sake, a restaurant full of people! But another part of her did not care if he undressed her right here and had his way with her on the very clean bar. And that part won out.

"Shhh," Aidan whispered, his lips brushing the soft flesh of her neck. She tilted her head back, her body pleading for more. Nothing else mattered but right now.

Chapter 5

I should be clear up front that Jason is not my boyfriend. I hate to call him a friend with benefits because that brings to mind hot twenty-somethings grinding their fit, toned bodies together in nightclub bathroom stalls. It does not conjure up lonely, flabby, middle-aged people getting together for the occasional necessary, if not altogether satisfying, lay.

I met Jason through a personal ad I can still barely admit to placing. I mean, how degrading is it to tell the world, albeit anonymously, that you can't find anybody to fuck you? It's the adult version of being picked last for the kickball team in gym class. But it had been almost five years. I lived in constant fear of waking up, looking in the mirror, and seeing a shriveled-up prune looking back at me. I was desperate.

"SDF, 46, mother, 5'4", curvy. Looking for an uncomplicated relationship. Friday late morning best. Disease free. Non-smoker. Fetishists need not apply."

I put the last bit in to be funny, but on some level I was being honest. The possibility of ending up with a man who wanted to talk dirty to my toes was even more depressing than being a prune. I needed to hedge my bets if I was going to survive this.

A man named Jason Blair responded to my ad. If his e-mail personality didn't exactly leap off the page, at least he didn't appear to be an ax murderer. We met for lunch two towns over, where I was happy to discover a somewhat attractive man attached to the name. Jason was forty-four, divorced, and worked as an intellectual property attorney in the city. He was passionate about model trains and DIY home projects, although he was currently living in a condo that did not require him to do more than change the occasional lightbulb.

He had brown hair peppered with gray, hazel eyes behind frameless glasses, and a small goatee that I hoped, if we ended up naked together, I could eventually talk him out of. His off-the-rack suit bunched up at the shoulders, and the lower buttons of his pale blue oxford strained against a burgeoning belly. The thought of that belly banging into mine left a bitter taste in my mouth. What was wrong with me? Why couldn't I just date like a normal divorced, fat single mother?

I'll tell you why. Because it's a desert out there, populated only by the damaged and desperate, of which I am one. After making this discovery, I bought a vibrator, but the way I went through batteries, I was becoming a one-woman ecological disaster. I needed the human version. Enter Jason. This was, after all, about fulfilling basic needs, not about launching a love affair for the ages. I was not looking for the man of my dreams. He did not exist. I was looking for sex. And that was something I would make perfectly clear to this nice man before any clothes were removed.

Jason reported he was here because his long marriage, which came to an abrupt end when he caught his wife in bed with the tile contractor, had left him with no confidence. He didn't know how to date or how to talk to women or how to have sex with anyone but his now ex-wife. He wanted to dip a toe back in the pool. I was the pool. After lunch was done, we had an awkward conversation that went something like this.

"So, um, well, what do you think about some sort of, ah, arrangement?" I asked. I was pretty sure Jason met my requirements. I could overlook the goatee for now.

"I don't know," he said. "I think maybe it could probably sort of . . . work. Right?" There was that confidence he'd mentioned.

"Yes."

"So we're agreed?" he asked.

"Yes," I said. "But it has to be Friday mornings around eleven thirty because that's when my housekeeper is out shopping for groceries and my daughter is at school."

"What did you say you did for a living?"

"I'm a writer. Novels. An author."

He didn't ask for titles.

"Okay. So next week, your place?" he asked.

"Great," I said.

"Oh and here," he said, handing me an envelope. "I'm disease free." Inside was a note from a doctor whose name I recognized, stating that Jason Blair was not harboring any sexually transmitted diseases and was not HIV positive. My new friend came with his own warranty. How nice.

"Thanks," I said. "I'll do the same for you." I already dreaded the conversation I was going to be forced to have with my internist.

We stood up and gave each other air kisses. It seemed a strange way to part from a man I'd just penciled in to fuck in a week's time.

Seven days later, as scheduled, Jason showed up at my house. I was nervous. I'd waxed and scrubbed and buffed and considered liposuction in the interim week, not that any of it made much of a difference. I reminded myself this was real life, and in real life, sex was much more ridiculous than in novels or in the movies. You could count on bad lighting and fat and sweat and awkwardness. But still, a part of me hoped it would be a transcendent experience. Or at the very least, distracting.

It wasn't transcendent. Just so you know. Jason brought me a limp bouquet of flowers from the Trader Joe's a mile away. It was nice but unnecessary. As Julia Roberts said in *Pretty Woman*, I was a sure thing.

"Come in," I said, stepping aside. Jason entered the large foyer, and immediately I began to question my own intelligence.

Who was this stranger I'd just invited into my house? Perkins wandered up, sniffed Jason's shoe, and wagged her tiny tail. So the dog liked him. That was something.

"I'm nervous," Jason said with a twitchy smile. "Isn't that crazy?"

I exhaled. "No, not at all. Me too."

"But I gotta get back on the horse," he said. My eyebrows shot up.

"No, no, no," he said, turning red. "I didn't mean to imply you were a horse . . . you're . . . very . . . pretty. Jesus. I'm sorry."

I laughed. This was absurd, all of it, but the only way through it was through it.

"It's okay," I said. I reached out and took his hand. It was damp and warm. I reminded myself not to be judgmental. After all, I had several spare tires around my middle, plus razor burn. The worst Jason had done so far was to compare me to a farm animal.

"Let's go upstairs," I said, suddenly bold. Was it the home-made granola Greta had forced on me that morning or the manifestation of pure desperation? As I lead Jason toward my bedroom, I decided not to question it.

"Your house is great," he said as we climbed the stairs. "What did you say you do for a living?"

"I write books."

"Right." Again, he did not ask for titles. If, by some strange twist of fate, Jason turned out to be Superman in bed, our relationship was still doomed. A man who reads is profoundly sexy. A man who does not is just some guy.

I'd made my bed that morning, afraid Jason would judge me a slob if I left it undone as usual. But pulling back the covers to reveal the clean pale pink sheets underneath was oddly intimate, like I was giving the guy a Sharon Stone–style glimpse between my legs. My face grew hot, and my heart, relatively calm until this moment, began to pound.

"Here, let me help," Jason said, yanking a blanket down to the foot of the bed.

"Thanks." Now what?

"Can I kiss you?" Jason asked. He wiped his palms on his pants. He was in worse shape than I was.

"Please," I said, stepping toward him. He smelled good, like breakfast. Coffee, pancakes, warm syrup. I reminded myself I was not here to eat him.

His lips were fine, not too dry, and fortunately he didn't slobber all over my face. I pulled back after a moment.

"Do we need to, like, set parameters?" I asked. Damn. I'd meant to do this downstairs. "Is there anything you really like or hate?" My face was beet red now, and there was no way to hide it. What an all-around bad idea this was. What sort of idiot thinks she can just dial up some guy and have inconsequential sex with him? I wanted off the bus.

"Well," he said. "I'm fond of blow jobs, but what man isn't? I don't generally do anal unless it's something you really enjoy. Having the lady on top is nice." He shrugged his shoulders. "I'm afraid I'm not exactly sexually cutting edge. I was married to the same person for twenty years. How about you?"

I stopped myself before I blurted out something along the lines of "Oh my god I just want to be touched by someone other than my daughter. I don't care how! I don't care where!"

"I'm with you," I said. "Nothing too kinky sounds fine. So how do we . . . um . . . do this? I mean the clothes part?"

"Well," Jason said, clearing his throat. "I'd love to take your clothes off, if that's okay?"

"Sure."

He did a nice job removing my garments. I'd made an effort to wear clean underwear with intact elastic, and even though my bras now resembled body armor as opposed to sexy lingerie, I'd chosen one with a little flower embossed between the cups. As he unclasped my bra and my breasts hung loose, I was again amazed at how big they'd become. I never envisioned myself as the proud owner of such a saggy pair of knockers.

But Jason liked them, burying his head in the folds of flesh and making weird sounds. Some men cared not so much about perky as about large. I tried not to think about the noise and just enjoy his soft hands lingering along my ample waistline.

When he was done removing my clothes, I asked politely if I could return the favor. The hair covering his chest was darker than what was on his head and flecked with gray. Was it discouraging as a man to see your chest hair go gray? If our relationship lasted longer than this morning, I thought I might ask him. Overall, I didn't mind hairy men as long as I was not required to rub sunscreen all over them.

Jason didn't have muscles, but his soft flesh was cool to the

touch and a nice olive color that spoke of a Mediterranean an-
cestor somewhere in the mix. I undid his belt buckle and dropped
his pants in a heap at his feet. Slowly, I reached my hands into
the waistband of his boxer shorts and gave those a tug.

The word *penis* is a no-no in erotic fiction. Choose some
other word: *manhood, member, hardness, cock,* whatever, but do not
say *penis.* It's a buzzkill. But in the real world, I say call a penis a
penis, and Jason's penis was just right for my purposes. Not too
big, not too small. It didn't veer off to one side in an inelegant
fashion or droop when it should be ready for action. Silently, I
applauded my still intact ability to make a man hard.

"Well," Jason said, gesturing toward the bed. "Shall we?"

I'd never been in this bed with anyone but Allison. Following
my divorce, I put all my bedroom furniture out on the curb with
a sign reading FREE. I wanted a clean slate. The old stuff was
gone within the hour, and I replaced it promptly with new stuff.
Different stuff. *My* stuff. And now I was about to lie down on my
stuff and allow a total stranger to cover me with his hairy body.

His weight made me groan. Men were heavy. This was something I'd forgotten.

"I like to be on top," I whispered. "But maybe this first time
we should, you know, just stick to the basics?"

Jason nodded. Beads of sweat dotted his forehead. Although
I knew he was not going to give me chlamydia or something
worse, I had no idea about his cardiovascular health. I tried to
relax, but I was dry as a bone. As Jason kissed my breasts and
my flabby tummy, I imagined being naked with George Clooney,

which was not as much help as it usually is. But Jason was going for it anyway. He wiggled his hips into position.

"Now?" he asked politely. We'd been in bed for all of three minutes. Oh well. Maybe I'd get the ice-cream-sundae version next week.

"Sure," I said. "But hold on."

I licked my fingers and ran them over the desert down below. Lubrication by any means necessary.

"Okay," I said. "Now."

Jason entered me like a thirsty man finally handed a glass of cold water. He groaned and shuddered and yelped out some *oh, oh, ohs*, and after about ninety seconds he collapsed on top of me with a single great heave.

"Wow, Sadie," he said when he caught his breath. "That was great."

I could think of a lot of words for it. *Great* was not among them.

When I didn't say anything, he slithered off me, propped himself up on his elbow, and studied my face.

"You didn't come."

In the four and a half minutes of sexual relations we'd just had? No. Not exactly.

"Well, no," I said. The upside of this relationship was there was no need to lie. This was not about feelings or emotions, so I did not have to be mindful of protecting either.

"Can I go down on you?" Jason asked with such sincerity I giggled.

"It's okay," I said. "I appreciate the offer. Maybe next time?"

We had to wrap this up before Greta came home and caught me naked in bed with a stranger before lunch. Jason's face showed relief. For a second I thought it was because he didn't have to dive down into unfamiliar territory. But it wasn't that. It was relief that I wasn't dismissing him for having the sexual control of a fifteen-year-old. He'd won another chance.

"I'd be honored," he said. And I giggled again. I couldn't help it. The giggling rapidly turned to laughter, and soon Jason and I were completely hysterical on my bed. Hysterical, naked, and sticky. I was still wiping the tears from my eyes as I got dressed. We parted at my front door with a brief kiss on the lips and a hug.

"Same time next week?" he asked.

"Yup."

"And I'll bring a wrench."

I stepped back. "A what? I thought we said . . ."

He smiled. The smile lit up his face.

"Your bathroom faucet leaks," he said. "I could hear it. I'll tighten it up for you."

I nodded. Great. A screw and a tighten.

"And I promise the sex will be better," he added. "I won't be nervous."

I nodded again. I was confident he could fix my plumbing, but as far as making me scream in ecstasy? We would have to wait and see on that one.

But it did get better. Quite a bit better. By week five, Jason

had figured out that if he wanted to coax an orgasm out of me, he had to do some work with his tongue. He told me he was amenable to instruction when it came to performing oral sex. So I took him up on it and provided step-by-step directions on what to do, when to do it, and where.

I wanted my ice cream sundae.

Chapter 6

Stolen Secrets
Chapter Three

Aidan Hathaway's fingers moved in slow circles on her back.

"The bartender," Aidan whispered in her ear. His hand returned to the back of her neck. Having it there made her feel weak and out of control. It was not something she savored, but she felt powerless to object. "Do you like him?"

What? Why was he asking her about the bartender?

"He seems fine," she whispered. His grip on her neck tightened.

"Do you want him?"

"I don't understand," Lily said. A cold bead of sweat trickled down her back. He pulled her closer.

"Do you want to fuck him?" His whisper was now

more of a growl. Lily's heart raced. What was this all about?

"No," she stammered. "I don't even know him."

"And?"

She had no idea what Aidan was after.

"I want you," she said finally, hoping it was the right answer. His grip on her neck relaxed.

"I want to see you naked," he said, matter-of-fact. "Let's go."

Normal people didn't do this. Normal people paid for their drinks and exchanged pleasantries with the maître d' on the way out. But not Hathaway. He did not come from the world of normal people. Did he know she was a girl who grew up in a house where the heat only worked when it wanted to? Did he know her dress was a knockoff and that half her paycheck went to support her mother? Lily imagined he did not. He would never be here with her if he did.

Aidan wrapped her in his arms, shielding her from everyone else in the bar as they made their way toward the door. Lily felt off balance from the exchange about the bartender. Could Aidan Hathaway be a jealous man? She didn't think it was possible for the person who had everything. What was there to be jealous of? But now her excitement at his proximity, at his touch, was laced with fear. Aidan was a man of grand appe-

tites. She was not at all sure she could satisfy them and survive intact.

Her instinct told her to run, to make some excuse and get free of him. She could get another job. She could move to another state, another country if necessary. As they walked, Aidan's hand slid deeper into the open back of her dress. Outside, the cool air hit her like a freight train. The sidewalk bustled with busy New Yorkers, coming and going, meeting each other, hugging, laughing, talking on the phone. Not one of them could possibly understand how she was burning up with lust for this strange, beautiful man. She pushed in closer to him, keenly aware of his hand inside her dress and against her skin. He smiled and kissed her, working his way under her bra just as he had done in the elevator Her body remembered. She wanted to cry out.

"Be patient," he said, pulling back. "Can you do that?"

She would do anything if it promised some release from the perfect painful pressure that was steadily building inside.

Aidan waved a hand, and a black Bentley with tinted windows pulled curbside. Would he wait until they got to his place, or would he rip her clothes off in his limo? The anticipation was a tight knot in her throat.

Just as Aidan was about to open the car door for her, an elegant older woman sprang from the backseat. She wore a skintight black dress, knee-high leather boots, and a gauzy black cape. Her inky, dark hair was pulled back from her face, highlighting her round, dark eyes.

"What the hell?" Aidan said. "Thomas!"

A liveried driver jumped out of the car.

"I don't know where she came from, sir," Thomas stammered, staring in shock at the woman. "One minute the backseat was empty and the next this . . . this person was sitting there. As if she appeared out of thin air! I'll call your private security."

The woman stood on the sidewalk, looking rather unconcerned as Thomas pulled out his cell phone and dialed. She smacked her cherry-red lips as if she were preparing to eat someone. She looked Lily up and down, lingering on the very spot where Aidan's hand was flush against her skin.

"They're four minutes out, sir," Thomas said.

"It's going to be a very long four minutes," the woman said, taking a step toward Aidan. She drank him in as if she'd been thirsty for a long time.

"You don't remember me," she said. It didn't sound like a question.

"I have no idea who you are," Aidan said gruffly, "or what you were doing in my car."

"You know my name," the woman said. "Clarissa."

"I don't know anyone named Clarissa."

"Oh but you do," she said. "You must!"

Clarissa did not believe for a moment that Aidan didn't remember her. They had shared too much to forget. Time and distance could not break them. They had love, and that was the only thing that mattered.

But then who was this tart with her dress half off standing beside her man, looking scared? As Aidan drew the girl protectively to his side and the chauffeur tried in vain to dial for help, Clarissa walked in a small circle around them. She did not know what Aidan could possibly be thinking. Couldn't he see this redheaded girl was not for him? He deserved so much more. He deserved Clarissa.

Aidan went quiet as she circled. He looked like a man under a spell. Quickly, the girl untangled herself from him.

"Excuse me," she said. "I should probably go."

"Lily, wait!" Snapping out of it, Aidan reached to grab her. His fingers locked around her upper arm. Clarissa had envisioned her reunion with Aidan many, many times, but none of the scenarios included a tall girl named Lily. Things were not going exactly as she had planned, and that made her angry.

Before anyone realized what was happening, Clarissa had pulled Lily into an embrace. She held her tight and muttered a chant. It was one she hadn't used in quite some time, but she knew it still had power. The air turned earthy, smelling slightly of char. In her arms, Lily labored to breath. She twisted, but Clarissa was too strong and Lily's will was too weak.

The night grew cold. Clarissa chanted faster. She could feel a climax coming, the moment of release. It was one of her most favorite experiences, and she relished it each and every time. But just when she saw success on the horizon, Aidan wrenched Lily from her arms.

"I don't know who you are or what you think you're doing," he growled, "but you're fucking with the woman I love, and I don't appreciate it."

Even as shock at his words threatened to break her, Clarissa still managed to register Lily's surprise at Aidan's proclamation. Perhaps "love" was news to the ginger-headed girl as well? Not that it mattered. None of it was okay. It could not stand.

Clarissa took a step toward them, close enough so she could run her long fingers through Lily's luscious curls. She gave a quick jerk. Lily gasped in pain. Aidan shoved Clarissa back, but a handful of red strands caught between her fingers.

"You need to go now," he said, "before I hurt you." His voice was low and fierce, but Clarissa just laughed.

"You belong to me, Aidan," she said.

"You're crazy," Aidan said.

"Sir, security is on the way," Thomas said. "Five minutes out."

"In five minutes, a few men won't be enough to save you," she whispered, holding Lily's strands of hair between her palms.

"A dark New York City," she said, her eyes fixed on Lily. "A place where you'll be alone." She hadn't done this particular spell in a long time, but it felt good.

"What are you doing?" Aidan demanded. How like the Aidan she remembered! Always standing up for the little guy, the downtrodden. But she had to show him what he had forgotten. There was no alternative.

Clarissa did not answer. She spoke faster, the words flowing from her lips like a waterfall in the spring. Suddenly, an invisible hand seized Lily and began to shake her violently. Her body quaked and shuddered. She screamed in agony, falling into Aidan's arms.

"Aidan, help me!" Lily screamed. Clarissa kept chanting.

"What are you doing?" Aidan shouted. "Stop!" He tried to lunge at Clarissa, but with Lily still convulsing in his arms, it was impossible.

And then there was silence. Lily had vanished.

Aidan staggered, the force of her disappearance practically knocking him off his feet. Clarissa stood in a pool of light cast by the overhead streetlamp, her diamond hoop earrings sparkling like stars, wearing a look of absolute rapture.

Aidan grabbed her shoulders and shook her hard. It did nothing to wipe the bliss from her face.

"Tell me what you did with Lily or I'll kill you," he said. "Right here. Right now. And I don't care who sees me do it." Clarissa was short on time. She'd delayed Aidan's private security detail as long as possible, but in a minute they would show up and complicate things.

"Oh, Aidan," she sighed. "You're really slow sometimes."

"I love Lily," he said. "I don't know who you are or what you've done, but it doesn't matter. You can't change what I know to be true."

Clarissa sneered at him. "Pathetic," she said.

"It's my destiny, you crazy bitch," he said. "And you cannot stand in the way of destiny."

"What does that even mean?" Clarissa said.

"Everything," Aidan said. "And I will do anything to get Lily back. I'll never stop."

Yes, she had planned there to be talk of love and destiny, but hers and Aidan's, not that of some girl named Lily. Clarissa decided to help her man see that Lily did not love him. She would help him see that his true destiny was to be by her side, doing her bidding. Because in her book, possession and control were the very definition of true love. Otherwise you were in for nothing but heartbreak.

"So you would risk your own life to save this woman?" Clarissa asked.

"Yes," Aidan said, without hesitation.

"And you're sure she wants something more than just

your pretty face and hard cock for a few hours in the dark?"

The fleeting look of doubt on Aidan's face pleased her. He had no idea how Lily felt about him. Until the words were spoken, until "I love you" was answered with "I love you too," it was all conjecture.

"Yes," Aidan said.

"Well then," Clarissa said, "why don't we find out if it's true?"

Right there in the middle of the sidewalk, she began to move her hands as if she were about to break into an exotic belly dance. Her black cape swirled around her. She looked terrifying. As her eyes rolled back in her head, a silent chant cascaded from her lips. A crowd gathered. Was this a street performance? Some sort of magic show? When her trance ended she leveled a triumphant glare at Aidan.

"I offer you this deal," she said. "I'll give you forty-eight hours to find your Lily and figure out the magic that will get you two back here. If you succeed, you get your Lily and my life. But if you fail, I own you forever. Will you accept my terms?"

The sirens grew louder, but at least her boy had the sense to understand his security could offer him no help on this matter.

"Yes," Aidan shouted as if on cue. "I accept!"

Clarissa stepped forward and laid a cold hand on Aidan's cheek.

"Somewhere foreign for you, my dear," she whispered, "somewhere beyond recognition. I only hope I can hit the target."

Aidan gulped for air, clutching his throat. He fell to his knees on the sidewalk. He tried to cry out, but it was too late. He vanished.

Clarissa stood for a moment, watching the spot Aidan had just occupied. And then she smiled.

Why should I miss out on all the fun? she thought.

Why, indeed. With a simple wave of her hand, Clarissa, too, disappeared into the night.

When security arrived on the scene moments later, they found Thomas on his knees, blubbering like a baby.

Chapter 7

Not five minutes after dropping Allison at school, I'm back in the minivan, heading across town to Target. I once considered starting a blog just so I could post an entry called "When Minivans Happen to Good People."

I live in Billsford, New York, a charming hamlet located about forty miles from midtown Manhattan. Our proximity to the only island that matters make real estate prices unreasonable and taxes so high the suicide rate climbs a few percentage points every April 15.

I forced the move from city to supposed country because one day, shortly after Allison was born, I tripped over a dead man in the entryway to our building, a great prewar place near the corner of Broadway and Great Jones. The police assured me the man had not died at the hands of another but rather from neglect and an unwillingness to take his meds. While this was marginally better than murder, I could not get the man out of my head. His dirty clothes and yellow, rotted teeth. His bare feet. His overall deadness.

"I donate to Pathways to Housing," I shrieked at the nice policeman. "I give bags of groceries to City Harvest. Why is this happening to me?"

"Well, ma'am, it's not exactly happening to you," the officer said. "He's the dead one."

The cop had a point. But still the dead man haunted me until my sleep-addled, hormone-bathed brain demanded action, the more illogical and dramatic, the better.

Bundling up an infant Allison, I hopped a Metro-North train and headed out of the city. I got off in Billsford because the train station was cute and behind it appeared to be a matching cute town. I wanted cuteness. I wanted green grass. I did not want homeless, forgotten dead people on my doorstep.

The real estate agent, sensing a live one, showed me five houses. They ranged from a ridiculous Tara-size mansion to a recently updated four-bedroom center-hall colonial. The lots were all multiacre, with gardens and trees and butterflies. I felt like I'd dropped into an early Disney film.

"You might occasionally see a wisp of smoke from a neighbor's hearth," the agent said to me. I had not heard the word *hearth* used in a sentence since we studied the Pilgrims in grade school. I liked it. I bought the house we were standing in at that moment, hearth, butterflies, and all.

Roger wasn't pleased. He wondered what sort of marriage we had if I didn't consult him about something as huge as moving out of New York City. I blamed my irrational behavior on hormones. Roger reminded me I was using that excuse for everything, which, I pointed out, did not make it any less true. I said he could buy a train pass and be at his SoHo yoga studio in under an hour. I told him he could expand and open another studio in chic Westchester County. The place had a whiff of rich, bored, well-maintained women. A gold mine. This made him a little happier, though not happy enough to remain heterosexual, I guess.

As I pull into a parking space roughly twenty yards from the doors of Target, I try to appreciate the upside of my suburban existence. There is always good parking to be found at the big-box stores on a weekday morning.

When I cross the threshold into the store, a blast of air-conditioned, artificial-smelling air escapes around me. The chill is welcome after the uncomfortable heat and humidity outside. On the short ride over, the radio overflowed with apoplectic weather reporters.

"Global warming!"

"Record-crushing heat!"

"Locusts!"

"Zombies!"

"Vampires!"

"The end of time!"

But to their credit, it *is* damn hot. I fumble around in my purse for today's shopping list, now amended with detergent and nail polish.

Hanging a left in front of the scarves and cheap handbags, I push an empty red cart in front of me. I miss the weight of my daughter in the small, flip-down seat, the way she would kick me relentlessly in the thighs as we traveled up and down the store aisles. After years of the constant presence of a small child, a solo trip to Target can feel downright bittersweet.

I turn in at the toilet paper and spend a full minute I will never get back considering which product to heave into my cart. Am I willing to wipe my ass with the equivalent of sandpaper and save the rain forests, or should I go with something that doesn't remove the outer layer of my epidermis upon application but will surely cause the downfall of human civilization? This is exactly how a trip to Target can end up taking all morning. I grab the two-ply store brand and push on toward the laundry detergent.

Out of the corner of my eye, I glimpse a man in Baby Products. He stands between a pink Pack 'n Play and a deluxe model ExerSaucer, decorated with a lot of sparkling stuffed fish. His arms flap at his sides like the wings of a baby albatross ready to take that first step off the cliff. With wild eyes, a flushed face, and bits of sweaty black hair stuck to his forehead, he looks insane. Which means I have no choice but to stop and stare. My cartwheels screech on the recently waxed floor. A loud voice interrupts the benign music to announce a special on beach towels.

"It's so hot outside," the voice says. "Stock up on these beautiful towels now!"

The man wears a dark custom-made suit over a starched white shirt and a red tie. The tie is too bright, the crimson unnatural looking. About halfway down his right leg, his pants are torn, revealing a wound encrusted with dark, dried blood. Mud cakes the bottoms of his Italian leather shoes, but somehow the mud is the wrong color, not quite earthy enough. Did he crawl through dried-out Play-Doh on his way here?

As I gawk, his arms slow down and finally come to rest at his sides. He spins in a slow circle, frowning, clearly confused to find himself surrounded by portable cribs and baby swings. He grabs one of the shiny fish from the ExerSaucer and rubs it against his grubby face. Pedophile? Lunatic? It doesn't matter, because I have actually stopped breathing. This man with the torn suit and the dirty shoes and the really weird relationship with toy fish might be the most beautiful person I've ever seen. My jaw hangs open like I left my IQ back there with the toilet paper.

Before any drool can actually escape, I close my mouth. Beautiful or not, this man is not having fun. He's in a bad way. Confused. He returns the fish to the ExerSaucer and runs his fingers roughly through his thick hair, twisting a longer front bit around and around until it seems he will pull the hair right out of his head. He winces and releases the hair, burying his face in his hands. He inhales deeply and repeatedly. When he finally looks up again, his eyes are calmer. He doesn't smile, but he no longer looks on the verge of an adult-size meltdown. He shakes out his shoulders, his arms, his wrists. He circles his neck a few times and bends down to touch his toes.

The suburbs are home to many weird people, believe me, but most of them are smart enough to practice their weirdness behind closed doors. It's safer that way. No one wants to play for Team Deviant.

I push my cart toward the man, who is now jogging in place. The fluorescent lights overhead pop and crackle with static. The tightness in my chest from this morning returns, mild enough that I don't fall to the floor gasping, but still, I'm aware of it. I rest my hand on my purse. The Xanax is in there if it gets any worse. This makes me feel much better.

"Excuse me," I say. The stranger is even better up close. His dark green eyes are framed by long lashes, the kind every mascara commercial promises to provide. His skin is clear and pale, like my marble countertops, but it radiates heat from within, giving him a rosy glow. He's young, twenty-five, thirty at the most.

"You're not planning on running a marathon in those shoes, are you?" I ask. The man startles like I just poked him with a cattle prod.

While he gives me the once-over, I have a moment to reflect on this morning's choice of clothing. My white T-shirt has moved across the color spectrum to dull gray, and my size 14 khaki skort, charming and carefree on the skinny catalog model, in reality resembles a potato sack. An unwashed ponytail, complete with aggressively split ends, does not help. I am the opposite of sexy. I am invisible.

"I don't run," the man says, looking down at his muddy

shoes. His luscious red lips turn up in an automatic smile not reflected in his eyes.

"Are you . . . okay?" I ask, taking a step closer. "It's just that you look . . . well, not so okay."

The man smells dusty, like mothballs, as if he was just taken out of storage. Up close, a faint white residue stands out against the dark fabric of his suit. He looks beyond me, off toward the dental hygiene aisle, as if trying to orient himself in space and time.

"Yes," he says. He goes for confident but misses the mark by a hair. "I'm fine. A rough start to the day, that's all."

On a typical weekday morning, the only shoppers in Target are moms or nannies. The suits, men and women alike, all got on the commuter train to the city hours ago. By now those suits have probably held two or three insanely productive meetings, made dozens of important decisions, had several cups of free-trade coffee, and squeezed in a quick game of squash at the New York Athletic Club. They are most certainly not standing around bewildered in Baby Products. A rough start, indeed.

"Is there anything I can *do* for you?" I ask. I have no idea what I will do if he says yes.

"Thank you, but I'm fine," the man says, straightening his tie. He glances at a Patek Philippe watch that, from the looks of it, is better suited for an expedition to the South Pole than one to suburbia. "Really. I'm okay. I appreciate your concern." His smile, now bright but still shy of genuine, indicates he'd like me to shove off. I can take a hint.

"Okay," I say. "Great. You have a nice day."

I begin to roll my cart away.

"Wait!" the man yells after me. His voice is just this side of frantic. "Would you please tell me what time it is? My watch appears to have stopped."

"Nine thirty-seven."

"And, well, I'm not sure quite how to ask this, but where exactly am I?"

What? I leave my cart and walk back. Standing directly in front of him, I gauge he is about six feet, two inches tall, with zero percent body fat. He probably comes by it naturally, too, which makes me like him a little less.

"Do you mean, where in the store or, you know, where in the universe?"

It's a question I don't think I've ever asked before. I wait while he considers his answer.

"I'd say more the latter."

"Oh."

"Yes."

"Did you have an accident?" I gesture to the hole in his pants. He glances down, surprised, and probes the wound with his fingers, wincing at the pain.

"I don't know," he says. "Maybe I fell?"

"Are you asking me?"

"I might be."

I should call 911 and tell them to pack a straitjacket. The man studies my face.

"Do we know each other?" he asks.

I'm experiencing the same sensation. He's familiar, but there is no way I'd forget meeting this guy.

"No," I say. "I don't think we do."

"Curious," he says.

"You're in Billsford, New York," I say. "Outside of New York City. Do you know what day it is?"

Again, he runs his fingers nervously through his hair. It stands up like porcupine quills. I can tell he'd hate knowing that.

"Billsford?"

"What's the last thing you *do* remember?" I ask.

He holds his hands out in front of him. He wants to tell me, to explain, but he comes up with nothing.

"I think I should call for some help. I'm concerned you may have injured yourself when you fell. Do you feel light-headed?"

"No," he says, looking around again. "But I do feel . . . strange."

Yes. That seems to be going around this morning. Perhaps he suffered a concussion? Or he's recovering from anesthesia?

"You haven't had surgery or played hockey recently, have you?" I ask.

"What?"

"Never mind."

"What is this place? What's all this stuff?" he asks.

"Target," I say.

"A target for what?"

That's the last bit of evidence I need.

"Can I please get you some help?" I ask. "Call someone?"

"No!" He grabs my wrist. A shot of heat races through my body from the point of contact. It's not lust but something different, some connection for which I cannot find the proper word.

"Oh my," I say.

He keeps a tight grip on my wrist.

"I want to go home," he whispers. His eyes search my face, and suddenly he reminds me of Allison, jolted awake by a nightmare, lost in the blurry place between reality and dreams.

"Of course you do," I say, peeling his fingers off my wrist. "Do you remember your name? Do you have a wallet?"

He obediently checks his back pocket and the inner jacket as well. Nothing.

"And I don't remember my name," he says as if this fact surprises him. What must it be like to forget that most basic fact about yourself? Who are you if you don't have a name? You're a blank slate. You're nobody. For some reason, this idea leaves me cold.

I walk the man toward the store manager's office. He comes willingly, shuffling his muddy thousand-dollar shoes along the floor. As I go, I dial 911.

Twenty minutes later, I hand the man over to an EMT with gray hair and a low, comforting voice. She inspires confidence. The man gives her a tentative smile. She takes my name

and address and phone number. Standard procedure, she says. And thank you for being a good, upstanding citizen. Okay, she doesn't exactly say that part, but I can tell she thinks it.

I turn to my new, crazy friend and smooth down his hair.

"You'll be okay," I say.

He looks skeptical but nods his head and returns his attention to the EMT as she slaps a blood pressure cuff around his arm. I am dismissed.

Only when I pull into my driveway do I realize I abandoned my cart with the carefully selected two-ply toilet paper somewhere near Baby Products.

Chapter 8

'm back home by eleven o'clock and seated at my desk. Although I hate to admit it, the Target man threw me. He was lost and confused and totally at the mercy of strangers. Relying on others for anything important is among my greatest fears. What if they fail you? Better to do what needs doing yourself and avoid the possibility of being let down altogether.

I probably could have survived the Target interaction with little drama, but layer on top fifteen hundred words appearing as if by magic in *Stolen Secrets* and you have the ingredients for a pharmaceutical intervention. I pop open the Xanax and toss back two little white pills. Some days are one-pill days, other days are two. Today is a two, and it's not even lunchtime.

I stare at my open computer screen. My hands tremble. Something very bad is happening. Probably a brain tumor. A psychotic break from reality. I remain in my chair perfectly still, and wait for the medication to kick in.

Chapter three was going just fine. Per my outline, Aidan and Lily were to leave the restaurant, go back to his place, and get naked in a slow and agonizing fashion. He'd tie her up and tease her, and she'd be shocked but ready. I knew *exactly* where this story was going when I went to bed. And there was nobody named Clarissa in it, that's for sure. Did my brain tumor slip me into some sort of creative trance? I throw back another Xanax for good measure. The doctor told me to mind my dosage because antianxiety medicine can become addictive, but right now I could not care less. A witch named Clarissa has hijacked *Stolen Secrets*.

A chirp from my cell phone interrupts the noise in my head. Jason is on his way.

I push back from the desk. I have twenty minutes tops until he arrives, and the least I can do for him is to smell like something other than anxious armpit sweat.

I emerge from the steamy shower still shaky, but it's not so bad that I can't control it. I'm wrapped in an orange towel when the doorbell rings. I peer out the side window and see Jason. He holds a bag of sandwiches from Vinnie's Italian Deli. Sometimes, if time allows, I let him stay for lunch and we have adult-themed conversations. You know, the lawyering gig, what movies we've seen, the housing prices in Billsford. Safe topics. Neutral topics.

But as I swing open the door, I'm almost overcome by the urge to tell him what a strange morning it has been. I'd start with the witch and head right on into the beautiful, crazy man in Target. But I stop myself short. We don't do that kind of conversation. We have sex and talk about the weather.

"Nice towel," Jason says with a smirk. These last months, Jason has gotten bold. He tells me he's dating. I lie and tell him I am too. Soon he will announce he has a girlfriend and our Friday mornings will be finished. I have yet to spend any time thinking about what that will mean for me. Or to me.

"I'm running late," I say.

Jason puts the sandwiches on a side table and yanks the towel. It falls to the floor.

"You have the best boobs," he says. "Handfuls."

"Gee, thanks," I say. "Upstairs?"

"You go first. I want to watch your naked ass walk up the stairs."

Jesus. I've created a monster.

A few months ago, Jason finally got around to asking me for the title of one of my books. Instead of explaining what *kinds* of books I write, I handed him the hardcover version of my latest K. T. Briggs effort.

"Bodice rippers?" he asked. He examined the cover, which featured a hot guy with long, flowing blond hair. His shirt was unbuttoned to expose a rippling six-pack, and he held a woman in his arms. She had the same flowing blond hair, but her eyelet dress was strategically torn to show creamy white thighs attached to long legs. There was a stallion in the background.

"In a way," I said.

"Can't wait to read it," he said. And boy, was he surprised when he did.

"You describe a nipple as an acorn!" he screamed at me the next week. "And a cock as a hard shaft of love!"

I shrugged. "So?"

"It gave me a hard-on, that's what. On the train. Embarrassing."

"You read it in public?"

"Well, I kind of wrapped it up in the *Wall Street Journal*."

"You need an e-reader."

"I guess. But I loved it. It was quite a read. I almost missed my stop."

"Thanks," I said. "That's nice."

"So do you, you know, do these things?" he asked.

I knew this question was coming, and I had my answer all prepared. Just because I write about something is not to say I practice it. I mean, I could write a biography of Abraham Lincoln never having met the man. Or a thriller about a serial killer without actually committing a murder. So why can't I write about leather boot fetishes without fondling my own footwear in a dark closet each night after sundown?

"No," I said, giving him the short version of an answer.

Jason caught himself just before his face registered disappointment.

"Well, maybe K. T. Briggs does them?" he asked.

I scowled at him for a moment. "She doesn't either. But it's nice you liked the book."

Jason came in less than a minute that morning. I'm sure he was thinking of me, or probably K. T. Briggs, shackled to the headboard, legs spread wide.

I walk up the stairs trying to keep my ass from jiggling, but it wobbles around back there like it's creating its own gravitational force. This idea makes me giggle. The earth and the moon and my ass.

The butt jiggle gets to Jason. We do it against the wall at the top of the stairs. He pins my hands above my head. It's awkward. Jason is probably five ten, but the height difference is enough that when he thrusts, he literally has to pick me up off the floor to get any leverage. I worry he will collapse from the stress.

"God, Sadie," he says, each time he slams me against the wall. "You feel so good today."

"I'm . . . glad . . . you . . . think . . . so," I say, in between thumps. There's a nice landscape by a local artist hanging to the right of my head. It bounces off the wall in perfect rhythm with the pounding. In this position, I swear I can feel his penis touching my molars. Standing up is not my favorite. I always end up longing for a footstool.

When we're done, we collapse on the hall carpet. It's a fairly new carpet, a pale green that works perfectly in this narrow space. Fern, I think it's called. I shift my body weight so gravity will keep the semen from running down my leg and staining the fern carpet. Jason runs a hand from my midsection down between my legs. He lets it linger there.

"So," he asks. "Your turn?"

Without waiting for an answer, he moves into position, spreading my legs so he can fit between them comfortably. My hip flexors strain. I start to relax. From here, I can see down the stairs and out the front door. Greta has watered the potted plants on the outside steps, but still they wilt in the outrageous heat.

Jason's tongue works its way from my knee toward the promised land. I have not yet come up with a way to tell him that licking my knee is a waste of good saliva. I have very few nerve endings in my knee. But apparently, that is where he has determined he should start, and I do not want to come across as ungrateful. His tongue is warm, and I close my eyes. I like the part right before his tongue plunges in. The anticipation, the promise, knowing the good stuff still awaits.

And there I am, ready for the good stuff, when the phone rings. Jason's head pops out from between my legs like a gopher's.

"Do you need to get that?"

No. I really don't. I want to stay here and enjoy your tongue making loopy circles around my clitoris until I cry out and pull your hair.

"Allison was sick last week, right?" he adds.

Jason remembering things like Allison being sick feels intimate in a way that bothers me, like a fingernail cut too short. But he's right. I have to answer the phone. There will be no promised land today.

"Shit," I sigh. I stand up, none too gracefully, and dash for the phone.

"Good morning," a chipper voice says. "This is Billsford General Hospital emergency services calling."

I stop breathing because when a hospital calls, it can only mean your child is dead.

"Is this Sadie Fuller?"

"Yes," I squeak.

"We have a man here who claims you are next of kin?"

"A man?" The air rushes out of me. I'm covered in goose bumps. Allison is not a man. But I have no brothers or uncles or nephews that fit the bill either. The goose bumps return.

"Is his name Roger?" I ask. "How old does he look?"

"Young," she says. "Probably twenty-five or so. And I don't know if his name is Roger. That's part of the problem."

Roger is very attractive and very fit. He can stand on his head for days. But he looks at least forty. Although I regularly tell him he can still pass for thirty-two because I want him to be happy.

"So you don't know his name?" I ask. "And he doesn't either?"

"No," she says. "He appears to be suffering from memory loss, but he remembered you well enough. Name, phone number, and address. He was brought in this morning. Really good looking."

She sounds embarrassed by that last bit, but now I know it's the Target guy.

"Can you tell us his name?" she asks. "Does he sound like someone you know? He even described what you look like."

How sad for me. It's hard to get away with dressing like a slob in a place like Billsford. Someone is always around to bust you. I'm about to say I have no idea who the man is, that I stumbled upon him looking dazed and confused in Baby Products and did my civic duty and that was that. But something stops me, some sense that I should go and see him.

"I'm not sure who you're talking about," I say, "but why don't I stop by there and see?"

"That would be great, Ms. Fuller."

We hang up. I'm still naked. Jason comes down the hall wearing only his boxer shorts. After I hit size fourteen, I no longer wanted to be naked in front of anyone, including myself. I was sure Roger found me unattractive and that was why our sex life had vanished. At least when he told me he was gay, I stopped blaming my new voluptuousness for our lack of physical contact. The problem wasn't fat, the problem was me being a girl, and there was no way around that. Jason, on the other hand, appears to experience only delight when he sees me without clothes.

"Everything okay?" he asks.

"Yes," I say. For some reason, it feels important not to share the details. I can't say why.

"Do you want to pick up where we left off?"

Both Jason and I have gotten rather adept at discussing sex like a business transaction. Did you get what you needed? How

did that work for you? Have we achieved any significant milestones? I tell myself it's fine, the modern approach to getting what you need.

"You know," I say, crossing my arms against my naked chest, "I think I'm good. I have a deadline looming that I should probably get on."

"Oh," Jason says. He sounds disappointed but recovers quickly. "I'll leave the turkey and sun-dried tomatoes for you. I think there might be provolone in there too."

"Thanks," I say, and I mean it.

Jason brings me sandwiches with cheese. He's kind and good-natured. I can admit at least that much without breaking my vows of no emotional attachment. He's not a greedy man. In fact, he doesn't seem to have a selfish bone in his body. He fixed my sink and my garage door opener and the back screen that kept falling off its hinges. And I think he might be losing weight. He claims he feels happy for the first time in almost twenty years. When he says that, I cry for no reason other than it is monumentally sad.

As Jason pulls his clothes back on, he talks about his new car, a sporty red coupe with black leather seats. I have no clothes, just a towel at the bottom of the stairs, so I excuse myself to get dressed. We meet a few minutes later at the front door. Jason is definitely skinnier. He looks good. I wonder if he knows it.

"Next week?" he asks. He always asks. It's part of our routine.

"Yup," I say, distracted.

He kisses me, and I more or less shove him out the door. The mystery of the good-looking man gnaws at me. I'm sure he got my name and number when I gave them to the EMTs, but why would he claim to be my next of kin? What does he want?

Five minutes later I'm in the minivan, headed for Billsford General Hospital.

Chapter 9

The minivan and I cruise along Billsford's narrow, curvy roads. The trees are lush and green, heady with springtime, and their branches hang low, making it impossible to see around the next bend. The hospital is not far, but getting anywhere in this town takes forever. I experience a pang of nostalgia for sidewalks and subways.

The hospital parking lot is full, and while I feel bad taking a space labeled "Patients Only," obviously intended for someone who is bleeding to death, I don't have much choice. Besides, I won't be here long.

Behind the large reception desk is a nurse wearing a name tag. BRIDGET, in all capital letters, like a shout.

"Hi," I say. I'm aware that my hair is suffering from having been vigorously thumped against a wall not thirty minutes ago. The key is to own it and not blush.

"Can I help you?" asks Bridget.

"I got a call earlier about a . . . man," I say. "I'm Sadie Fuller."

Recognition on the part of BRIDGET.

"Of course," she says. "The guy. The good-looking guy."

"Yes."

"He's very attractive," she says again. She's young and pretty. I understand where she's coming from.

"Right," I say.

She returns to her professional senses, possibly shaking off an image of our subject in a flimsy, untied hospital gown.

"He's finishing a psych evaluation right now," Bridget says, glancing at her computer. "If you go up to the third floor, the duty nurse there can assist you."

I head to the elevator banks.

"He's really good-looking," Nurse Bridget yells after me. She's dying to ask if he's single and available, but they probably told her in nursing school that hitting on delusional patients was pushing the limits of good taste.

The third floor smells more like a hospital than the lobby did. A combination of antiseptic, bleach, and recycled air masks an underlying odor of sickness and misery. The fluorescent lights cast a greenish glow over everything. I've never found hospitals to be the sorts of places that inspire one to go on living.

Cathy is the duty nurse. She wears an old-fashioned nurse's

cap that makes me want to call her Sister and cross myself, just as a precaution.

"You don't have a badge," Sister Cathy says immediately, examining my chest.

"No," I say. "Bridget didn't give me one."

Sister Cathy tsk-tsks. A printer whirs to life, and a badge is procured.

"Now," she says, settling in behind her duty station and adjusting the nun's cap, "can I help you?"

"I'm here to see if I know the good-looking man," I say. It sounds ridiculous, but it's more or less the truth. Nurse Cathy narrows her gaze.

"You guys called *me*," I say. "I'm trying to help identify a patient."

"The good-looking one?"

Didn't I say that already?

"Yes. Do you have a lot of patients here who don't know their own names?" I ask.

She ignores me. "He's very . . . charming," she says. She busies herself on the computer, but there is no denying the faint bloom on her cheeks. She probably hasn't been this excited since the Pope celebrated Mass at Yankee Stadium.

"I'm sure he is."

"He's out of his psych evaluation now," she says brusquely, standing. "I can take you to see him."

A strange nervousness rises in my chest, a sense of anticipation mixed with dread. The patient is in a private room. Perhaps that is because he's the only patient up here, or maybe because Nurse Cathy thinks he's a babe. And charming. Sun floods in from a huge window and backlights him in such a way I think angels might start to sing.

Nurse Cathy sighs. "He's so . . ."

"I know," I interrupt. "Charming."

The man turns at the sound of my voice.

"Sadie," he says, rushing to me and taking my hands in his. Nurse Cathy watches us carefully. His eyes plead with me. His hands are cold in mine. He squeezes. Please.

"Harry," I blurt, possibly because I was gazing at Prince Harry on the cover of *People* magazine in the supermarket yesterday. I turn to Nurse Cathy, a big fake smile plastered on my face. "This is Harry . . . Plant. My second cousin once removed."

I sometimes wonder if anyone other than British royalty can make sense of that "removed" business, but I feel it makes my claim difficult to argue against.

"The rest of the family is across the pond," I say, warming up to my lie. A look of pure relief spreads across the newly dubbed Harry's face. I have no idea what I'm doing. Recently I read that helping others is the best way to feel good about yourself. Maybe I'm just taking that idea to an unusual extreme.

I hug Harry. His body is firm and lean. I feel muscles through his shirt.

"How are you feeling, old chap?" I ask. Nurse Cathy rolls her eyes.

"So you can identify this man?"

"Haven't I just?"

"I'm getting the doctor," she says, turning on her heel and marching out of the room.

Second cousin Harry sits down on the bed.

"Thank you," he says quietly. "I'm not sure I could have survived another minute in this place."

It takes my brain a second or two to catch up. Cousin Harry thinks I'm going to spring him.

"Oh," I say, sitting down beside him. "I'm not sure I can, or that I should, you know, take you out of here. You're not well."

He stands abruptly.

"I'm fine," he says. "I'm perfect."

"I know," I say soothingly. "But you can't remember who you are, right?"

He sits back down, deflated.

"No," he says.

I shrug to indicate I can't take a stranger with memory loss to my house. It just doesn't make any sense, all good intentions aside. He takes my hands in his again, moving in close to me on the edge of the bed. I experience a sharp moment of déjà vu.

"They served me canned peas," he says, looking viscerally offended. "And Jell-O. I've never seen food like that before in my life. I'm desperate. But they won't let me go unless someone vouches for me. You know who I am."

"No, I don't."

"Well, you just pretended you do."

"Okay," I say, "let's say, just hypothetically, I sign you out. Where will you go?"

"I'll go, well, I'll just head for . . . maybe I'll go to . . ."

"I think it's best if you stay here," I say. "Safest."

Cousin Harry slides off the bed and down onto one knee, as if he is going to propose marriage. He smiles. It's a beautiful smile, and I'm momentarily overwhelmed by its sheer loveliness.

"Please," he says. "There's something I must do. For the love of God, please help me."

"What is it?"

He falters but does not let go of my hand. "I . . . I can't remember exactly, but it's urgent. I can feel it. It's . . . love."

Well, that seals it. Generally speaking, if an apparently homeless, familyless man who cannot remember his own name starts muttering about love, it's time to call for a net because he is clearly loony tunes. Nothing against Bugs Bunny, but you know what I mean.

Yet there is something in his face that gives me pause, a radiating anguish that demands I pay attention and really consider his words. Before I can answer, the doctor walks in. He's young with round glasses and a mop of unruly hair. The black bags beneath his eyes indicate he's been here for days, perhaps even years, probably eating canned peas down in the cafeteria. He stifles a yawn with his fist. His eyes flutter. He's going to fall asleep on his feet right in front of me. I make a fast, illogical, and slightly ludicrous decision to get Cousin Harry out of here

before this exhausted doc accidentally removes his liver or his right leg below the knee.

"Doctor," I say. He startles. Behind him, Nurse Cathy glowers.

"Ms. Fuller," he says, studying his clipboard, trying to remember why he is here. "Nurse Cathy says you know our patient."

"Might know," Nurse Cathy corrects.

"Oh," I say, "I definitely know him. His name is Harry Plant. He's a second cousin. We practically grew up together."

Nurse Cathy snorts. "Old enough to be his mother," she says under her breath. Bitch.

The doctor sighs, and sways on his feet. He wants only to get this guy out of here so he can take five in the break room. And he's not going to let some batty old nurse derail him. With a wave of his hand, he dismisses Nurse Cathy from the scene.

"Mr. Plant doesn't appear to have anything wrong with him," the doctor says. "We fixed up his leg, but his CAT scan was clear. No brain trauma. I suggest you get him to his primary care physician as soon as possible and let them monitor the memory issue. My feeling is it will all return within the day. That's how these things usually go."

"I have total confidence in your decision, Doctor," I say. "I'll take care of him."

"It's great to have family," the doctor says.

"Isn't it?" I say, kicking Harry's shoes and socks in his direction.

"Well, just sign here and you're all set."

I don't bother with the fine print. I sign the release papers. I usher the relieved doctor out of the room and turn back to Harry. What have I just done?

While Harry works on the footwear, I panic. I fish around in my bag for my emergency Xanax, but apparently I've taken them all. Harry stands up and puts his arms around me in gratitude. He smells of hospital, which is all wrong. This man should smell like pine trees and money and sex.

"Thank you," he whispers into my messy hair.

I push him away. I feel tingly, like my whole body is a funny bone that just got whacked on the sharp corner of a table. I'm no better than Nurse Cathy.

"Let's go," I say.

I open the minivan side doors from across the parking lot. Cousin Harry freezes in his tracks.

"What is that?" he says.

"My car," I say.

"It's a . . . minivan," he says, making no attempt to disguise his horror.

"And?" My minivan is the same as an annoying relative. I can make fun of it, but you can't.

"It's just I've never been in one before," he says. It's fascinating to watch him attempt to regain his emotional footing.

"So I guess we've established that you don't have kids," I say. Although I could probably have deduced this same thing from how utterly out of place he looked at Target this morning. If you have kids, you can shop Target blindfolded. The store is an inescapable side effect of parenting.

"No," he says. I think he shudders. "I don't believe I do."

I toss my purse in through the open back door and slide it shut as I pull open the front passenger door. The seat is covered with empty coffee cups, pieces of unopened mail, a scarf, a plastic baggie with what might have been a peanut butter sandwich back in the Jurassic period. I pick the stuff up en masse and toss it into the back. My companion gasps.

"What are you *doing*?" he asks.

"Did you want to sit on all of that?" I ask. "Because I can put it back."

"No," he says, gingerly stepping into the minivan, "it's just that cars are like women. They must be respected, treated as beautiful. All of them."

It's the first moment since we've met that I think he might actually be crazy.

"It's a goddamn minivan," I say. "It doesn't deserve respect."

Cousin Harry grimaces.

"I drive a vintage Jaguar and a Maserati," he says suddenly. "I also have a Bentley, but that comes with a driver."

We both freeze and stare at each other.

"Where do you keep the cars?" I ask quietly, quickly.

He closes his eyes. "They're in a warehouse, I think," he says. "It's very . . . urban."

Well, that narrows it down to about twenty-five states.

"I'm sorry," he says. "I'm not being helpful."

I pat him on the arm. "It's great that things are starting to come back to you."

Confusion clouds his face.

"Check out the giant cup holders," I say, starting up the engine. "Bet you don't have room for twelve cups of coffee in your vintage Jag."

We pull out of the parking lot and I head for home because I have no idea what else to do.

Chapter 10

was born to write romantic novels. Even a cursory investigation of my childhood indicates I had no real choice in the matter. I grew up an only child in a small upstate New York town. My parents were older and both literature professors at the local liberal arts college. My mother wore flowing peasant skirts and lots of brightly colored beads. She had wide hips and big hands and a loud voice. Her long hair hung loose and free, and in the summertime, she occasionally tucked a mess of tiny daisies into it because, of course, her name is Daisy. Daisy floated along in life, a big, happy smile perpetually plastered on her face because she had my father, Walter. Tunic-wearing, bald-spot-sporting, Birkenstock-clad Shakespearean Professor Walter Fuller.

Walter loved Daisy more than anything under the sun and does, to this day. He anticipates her every need. He surprises her with shiny baubles, matcha green tea soy lattes, and exotic chocolates (Jalapeño! Cardamom!). Rumor has it Daisy couldn't handle changing diapers, so Walter managed to wipe my cute little ass every single time so his darling wife would not run the risk of swooning at the sight of baby poop. Walter exists to serve Daisy, and in return, Daisy showers him with love.

Professor Daisy Fuller's area of expertise is Jane Austen. I was weaned on a world of romance thwarted, only to be dramatically resurrected in the final chapters for a perfect happily ever after. And Daisy's own life seemed to illustrate this. After all, she met Walter when she was forty-two years old, and look how well that worked out? That love in the last quarter of the game happened only for Ms. Austen's characters and not for the woman herself did not matter to my mother in the least. She never once mentioned to me that the great romance author died alone and unknown, at age forty-one.

On cold winter nights, the three of us would sit in the small living room, as close to the wood-burning stove as we dared get, reading books. It was common, almost required, that when you got to a good passage, you read it aloud, assuming character voices as necessary. At breakfast, I was peppered with bits of sonnets and passages from *Pride and Prejudice*. My parents constantly quoted great white, dead authors to each other and then disappeared into the bedroom in a fog of lust, leaving me to play solitaire at the dining room table.

When we read *The Great Gatsby* for school my mother made a point of telling me how awful it was.

"But it's an American classic," I said. "It says so on the cover!"

"It misses the point entirely," she shot back.

"What point?" I begged her.

"*The* point," she said, and would not elaborate. Eventually, I came to understand she did not like sad endings. If the boy and the girl do not end up together, why on earth bother? And I tended to agree with her. After reading *Gatsby*, I walked around with an uncomfortable knot in my stomach. I'd absorbed these poor, wretched creatures into myself, and now I could not get rid of them. They haunted me, and the discomfort was such that at the young age of twelve or so, I decided Daisy's point was worth heeding. Go for the happy ending or die trying.

So it made perfect sense that I would write about love. If you go to the library and look up Sadie Fuller, you will find a number of fairly well-known contemporary romances. I wrote the kinds of novels that were considered "sweet," as in no heaving breasts or erect penises or orifices of any sort. I was very good at implying intimacy and leaving the sweaty mechanics to the readers' imaginations.

I banged out five or six of these books a year. One even reached that pinnacle of measurable success, a made-for-TV Lifetime movie. What constitutes a good story was baked into my bones. I could create a gauzy romantic scene at a NASCAR race, for God's sake, and that's an accolade not many can claim. I was making a living, paying my rent, and buying shoes I didn't need. And I was happy because I *believed* in romance. It was my one true faith. We all deserved flowers and diamonds and a man entirely devoted to our happiness like Walter was to Daisy. We were due our champagne and starry nights and kisses so deep they made us weak in the knees. Weren't we? I didn't consider my books fantasy or escapism. They were simply the fictional manifestations of what I knew was waiting for me just around the corner.

And one day I went around that corner and there was Kurt Allen. I remember the first words he uttered as though they were seared onto my brain with a branding iron.

"Excuse me, miss, but you dropped these."

I was twenty-nine years old, hoofing it downtown for a meeting with my literary agent. Although I was still seven months from hitting the big three-oh, my mother had begun making jokes about how I should get a cat to go with my spinsterhood. We laughed. She hung up. I cried. But now here was a man who could have been the model for Barbie's Ken, holding my keys and smiling down at me.

I heard angels. I saw stars. I was speechless.

"You dropped them a few blocks back," he said. "You walk really fast."

He wore a suit that did not come off any rack and carried a briefcase that seemed very grown-up. His leather shoes reflected the pale winter sunlight, and I had a sudden vision of him sitting at one of those shoeshine stations in Grand Central Terminal.

"Thank you," I stammered. He followed me! This beautiful man ran after me to make sure I got my keys back!

"My pleasure," he said. I regretted my black gloves as I

reached out to take the keys. I wanted to feel his skin, even just his fingertips. "Are you headed downtown?"

"Yes," I said. My voice still sounded shaky. I commanded myself to get a grip. This meeting was not mere chance. This was fate. This was destiny! I was already on chapter three of the novelization.

"Can I walk with you?"

It was as if a rose suddenly burst into bloom in my chest.

"Please," I said. "That would be nice."

As we made our way down the crowded sidewalk, Kurt Allen gave me his abbreviated biography. He worked for his father's law firm. He lived an upscale life at an uptown address. He was on his way to meet a friend for lunch but would be willing to re-schedule if I could see my way to rearranging my agent meeting.

What do you think I did?

We had a three-hour lunch. We sat in Union Square even though it was cold. He kissed me by the busy dog park. This turned out to be unfortunate because, as you know, the human olfactory bulb resides in a part of the brain closely associated with memory making. But I refused to see it as a sign that every-thing would eventually go to shit.

I studiously counted up five dates before I would take my clothes off for him, as some book I'd read suggested. When we finally did get naked, I discovered Kurt made love like a frat boy who is anxious to finish before someone kills the keg. I made excuses on his behalf because I already loved him. I saw us together in old age, sitting on the porch of some New England farmhouse, watching our grandchildren, holding hands.

Now Kurt didn't bring me flowers or chocolates or sparkly, shiny things just because he was bursting with joy at having me in his life. But I told myself I was not living in Jane Austen's England. I was a modern girl in New York City. I knew Kurt loved me. I could feel it.

After a year, he invited me to move in with him. It was the first time I'd lived in a place with a view of something other than the exterior wall of the building next door. I bloomed in the sunlight. I decorated. I picked out new towels. I hummed love songs. I didn't bother learning to cook because we went out or ordered in. We were so fabulously New York! Soon we'd be engaged and I could begin obsessing over flowers and a color scheme and what dress would best show off my deep brown eyes. At long last, I was experiencing what I spent so much time writing about. Can you feel me cringing?

So there I was, living my fantasy, busily working on a book about two young, fabulous New Yorkers canoodling at all the landmarks and buying towels together. I devoted my free time to telling everyone how wonderful love was. Finally, I'd been invited to join the club. But there were potholes in the road. Chasm-deep, chassis-bending potholes.

The first hole I fell into was a pair of black lace panties in the laundry that were not mine. It took me more than a minute to register their presence as alien, and when I finally did, I tried to talk myself out of it.

"Kurt doesn't go in for lacy lingerie," I said. "And he's not big on crazy sexual positions either. He likes it missionary. He's a traditional man." I mean, he would never consider coming into the bathroom when I was in there, brushing my teeth or taking a pee. There were certain lines he felt should never be crossed. But here I held a pair of black lace panties. I threw them in the trash. Maybe they belonged to Verna the cleaning lady? Sure. They might fit over her left ankle.

But I persevered in my delusion because I could not conceive of love gone bad. This was not *The Great Gatsby*. This was my fabulous life! And then I hit the second pothole, the distinct whiff of expensive perfume on my boyfriend's rumpled suit jacket. I immediately went to his enormous walk-in closet and threw the doors wide. A million fists of the same scent assaulted my nose. I backed up as if physically pushed. My perfume was far more flowery, girlie. This one was dark and sensual and made my eyes water.

The last pothole on my road to love and marriage, and really the only significant one, was all of my worldly belongings, neatly boxed up and waiting for me in the foyer of the beautiful, sunny apartment I apparently no longer shared with Kurt.

After two years together, Kurt Allen explained it away thus. "I really like you, Sadie, but you're not the type of girl I can marry. I need someone more serious. And maybe taller. It's important for my career." Or something like that. I'd stopped listening about halfway through his oration, the ringing in my ears so loud as to drown out all other sound.

In the following weeks, we met several times at Starbucks, the only place he'd agree to see me. I got the sense he thought a public place would prevent me from making a scene. Had I really become that kind of girl, the one who shrieks and rends her garments?

I tried to convince him he was throwing away something wonderful, but he was having none of it. He just kept repeating that I wasn't right for him, like a mantra. Our wonderfulness was clearly all manufactured. By me. I was left with several poorly packed boxes and a single question echoing in my head: how could I have been so wrong about Kurt?

Like a cliché, I took to my bed in the studio apartment I'd rented unseen. Drowning in pain and anguish, I had no idea what would come next in my life, nor did I care. I'd been kicked out of the happily ever after club, the only club I'd ever wanted to join.

After I'd spent a few months of concentrated moping and the missing of several important deadlines, my literary agent, Liz Stelow, suggested I expand the definition of romance in my work.

"Throw in a little sex," Liz said. "It's hot right now. BDSM. OTK. Visit a fetish shop. Take a class on how to play with needles. I don't care. Kink sells."

"OTK?"

"Over the knee."

I had to get out more.

"But really, Sadie, it's time to get off your ass," Liz said. "You're starting to irritate me."

I had never considered writing about sex. The mere idea made me blush. After all, I was fairly conservative in the bedroom. Wild was leaving the lights on. Perhaps that's what drove the love of my life into the arms of black lace panties and sexy perfume?

"Forget it," I told Liz. "I couldn't possibly."

"Come on, Sadie," she said. "All these love stories you write, you must think through the graphic details you don't include, you know, late at night? When you're alone? Or maybe you practiced them with that wretched man you're so much better off without?"

The mere mention of Kurt set off another round of crying, after which Liz promptly hung up on me. As I wept, I noticed an eventual absence of tears. After ten weeks, I had cried myself dry. I was shriveled up. Done. It was over. I laid my head on my desk in utter defeat.

But then came a voice. It sounded like me but stronger and much more sure of herself.

"Here's what you need to do," the voice said. "Put what's left of your romantic heart in a box. A nice box, maybe Tiffany blue or a soothing peach color, but strong, a container capable of hosting your ticker during its permanent quarantine from love-related endeavors. You are an independent, self-supporting woman. Now, step away from the box, stop irritating your agent, and write about something *else*."

"Yes," I said out loud to my empty apartment. "Love is just a genre. It's not a life sentence."

Wearing the same plaid pajamas I'd had on for a month, I shuffled to my laptop, blew the dust off the cover, and popped it open. Confronted with an empty document, I almost screamed, a bubble of panic rising in my throat, threatening to strangle me. The truth is, in publishing, if you can't produce, there are hundreds of others who can. I could feel their collective hot breath on the back of my neck. I placed my fingers on the keyboard. I relaxed my shoulders. Sex is physical. Writing about sex is the same as writing about baseball or martial arts or war. It happens. Describe it, Sadie. Describe the details. Don't leave anything to the imagination.

I ended up with several chapters about a superhot girl named Sally who fucks the brains out of a loser named Kurt and then dumps his ass because he's a jerk who just can't get the OTK right. Afterward, I felt as good as if I'd had every orgasm myself, so I kept right on going.

I wallowed in the language. I used tongues and teeth and throbbing cocks and masturbation while on public transportation. I used leather whips and handcuffs and nipple clips. There was spanking and bondage and domination. Everything was hot and wet and pulsing with desire. I bought the Kama Sutra and studied the pictures over my morning coffee. I used wine and molten chocolate cake to bribe sexual confessions from friends and acquaintances while I took detailed notes. I never would have guessed how many seemingly normal people wanted to have sex in the elevator of a skyscraper.

Less than a month later, I dropped a fully formed manuscript into Liz's e-mail box. She called me the very next day.

"God, Sadie," she said. "This made me so horny I had to call my husband and have him go down on me over the phone."

Fuck Jane Austen. K. T. Briggs had arrived.

Chapter 11

As we drive away from the hospital, I pepper Cousin Harry with questions.

"Does any of this look familiar?"

"No."

"You said this was about love. Do you remember why?"

"No."

"Are you married?"

"I don't know."

"Do you have a girlfriend?"

"I don't know."

"A boyfriend?"

He shrugs.

"So what *is* the last thing you remember?"

"A bar. A dark restaurant. Maybe sushi?"

"Are you asking or telling?"

He glares at me. I ease up.

"I'm going to take you to my house," I say. "I'm not sure what else to do with you."

"The cup holders are very nice," he says. "Perhaps if you cleaned her, she wouldn't make that noise every time you go around a corner."

"What noise?"

"Never mind. I'm sincerely grateful for your help. I'm sure I'll feel much better very soon."

I don't tell him, but I suspect I'll have him identified via the Internet way before that. Good-looking, custom-suit-wearing, chauffeur-driven guys are not a dime a dozen, you know, even in the tristate area. Somebody out there must be looking for him.

I pull the minivan into the garage at 32 Elm Road and shut the door before I click the lock release and allow my new houseguest to climb out. The lots here in Billsford are huge, but I know people use binoculars to spy on their neighbors. Yes, it's twisted, but people with a lot of money are often bored out of their minds, and spying gives them purpose. Neighborhood watch, they say. Just keeping the 'hood safe from . . . what exactly? Bears? Trolls? People with less than seven-figure incomes?

Cousin Harry does not fit in my house. It's a girls' house, populated these last five years entirely by females. It's light and airy, and there is no shortage of flowery furniture and drapes. In the wine refrigerator, we have Chardonnay, rosé, and a selection of decent Pinot Noirs. But we never have beer. If you want beer, you better bring your own. We put our shoes away. Our dirty laundry goes in the hamper. We never slobber toothpaste all over the sink, and our toilet seat stays permanently in the down position.

Harry frowns, like he can't quite fathom my house as an actual dwelling.

"I think I live somewhere up high," he says, looking around. "On the top floor maybe? A penthouse?"

This does not exactly come as a shock. In the kitchen, I gesture for Harry to take a seat at the table. Where is Greta? But more important, what the hell am I going to tell her when she turns up?

"Are you hungry?" I ask.

"I feel like oysters and champagne," he says. I laugh. He doesn't. I don't think he's kidding. I stop laughing.

"How about some leftover macaroni and cheese?" I ask.

"To eat?"

You'd think rescuing a guy from canned peas and Jell-O would garner a little gratitude, but apparently not.

"My German housekeeper made it," I say. "It's the best."

Harry must be on the verge of starvation, because he agrees to try it. Three bites in and there's a moan of pleasure. Greta's mac and cheese will do that to you. Before I advertised for Jason, I ate a lot of it.

While he swoons over his plate, I wonder how insane it would be to leave a total stranger alone in my house while I run off and get Allison from school. But Harry does not seem threatening. I feel as if I know him, and have known him, even though that's not possible. Plus he's in a fat- and carb-induced coma of sorts. How much trouble can he get into?

"I have to pick up my daughter from school," I say. "When I come back, we'll get busy on the computer and figure out who you are, okay?"

It takes him a second to come to, but he's clearly rejuvenated by the Greta calorie bomb. There's even a bit of pink in his cheeks.

"Okay," he says. "How do we do this picking up your daughter thing?"

I laugh. I can't help it. My cousin Harry was clearly born with a silver spoon in his mouth. As I laugh, Harry first smiles and then joins me. It's a wonderful sound, bottomless and full, and I experience it in my thighs as a quivery, tense sensation that overwhelms the circuits in my brain.

Lust. It's a feeling so unfamiliar it renders me momentarily speechless.

"Are you all right?" he asks.

"I'm fine," I say, standing up and fanning my face with a bit of German-language newspaper. "Suddenly hot."

How dreadfully embarrassing.

"Well, I did notice it's unusually warm out," he says.

"Yes," I say. "Practically steamy." I continue to fan my face. "Why don't you get cleaned up while I pick up Allison? There's a shower upstairs, two doors down on the left, fresh towels under the sink. I'll be back in a few minutes."

But somehow I've blown it, because from the way Harry eyes me, much has been revealed. I'm an open book. Or better yet, a tasty morsel. I don't believe I have ever been looked upon in this fashion.

"A shower sounds great," he says slowly, "but I think I have the answer to at least one of your questions."

"My questions?" My brain sizzles, possibly requiring measurement in Kelvin. If I were a cartoon character, steam would vent from my ears.

"In the car," Cousin Harry says, "you asked if I had a wife, a girlfriend, or a boyfriend."

He smiles. It's predatory and sarcastic, as if he is already laughing at what he is about to do.

"I'm pretty sure I don't have a boyfriend," he says, "because what I really want to do right now is hike that skirt up over your hips, bend you over this table, and fuck you until you beg me to stop."

My cheeks flare bright red. My stomach does a gold medal backflip off the high dive. Who talks like this? His eyes bore into me as he waits for an up or down vote. But all I can think is this guy has tried this approach before and met with success. He does not seem the type to attempt a failed line twice.

"It's a skort!" I blurt.

That takes a bit of the puff out of his sails. "A what?"

"A skort," I repeat. "Shorts and a skirt together. As one. So, you know, you can ride a bike or do cartwheels and not flash innocent bystanders." And hey, what about all that love business in the hospital? What happened to that?

"Show me," he says.

"What?"

"The skirt thing. The two-in-one."

It's a sincere request. He's never heard the word *skort* before. And why would he have? Skorts have no place in his penthouse, Bentley-limousine, thousand-dollar-haircut life. He waits.

This is all my fault. I felt lust and desire, and now I'm going to have to pull up my skort as punishment. I roll the hem of the awful khaki garment just enough to reveal the black cycling-style shorts beneath.

"A modern-day chastity belt," I mutter, eyes averted, as he studies the setup.

"I've never met anyone like you," he says with a curious smile. "You're . . . soft."

He stares at my midsection as he says this, and so help me God, I think seriously about smashing him over the head with the Pyrex of macaroni and cheese. Soft? Why do good-looking people think they can act like assholes and get away with it? Well, mostly because they can.

"I don't care if I'm *unique* in your experience," I say. "I'm still not going to let you pull down my skort."

He shrugs. "I had to try," he says.

"Go and get cleaned up," I say.

And with that last directive, I grab my keys and flee the house, the flames that just consumed my last shred of dignity nipping at my heels.

Chapter 12

I drive the route to Holt Hall so often, I can practically do it with my eyes closed. Which is a good thing, because right now my concentration is completely shot to shit. I'm sweating, and the skort, usually the pinnacle of comfort if not glamour, feels itchy and constricting.

I have a number of friends, but I don't run with a mommy posse or claim a BFF as some around Billsford do. When I'm faced with a crisis, I usually call Roger. This is partly reflex and partly laziness. Roger knows my backstory. He doesn't require lengthy explanations for my behavior.

He answers on the third ring.

"Oh God," he says, panting. "I was trying to recite the words to 'Instant Karma' while in a headstand. It made me dizzy."

"Hi, Roger," I say. "Busy?"

"No." Of course he's not. Roger is never actually busy.

I explain briefly about Cousin Harry. I leave out the part about him wanting to fuck me on the table. I don't see how sharing that detail will be helpful. There is a long pause, during which I can hear Roger pursing his lips.

"What," he says after a moment, "is *wrong* with you, Sadie?"

A lot of things. Many things. But I don't think that is what Roger is asking.

"You're the one who gave me that book about feeling good by helping people in need," I shoot back.

"Nowhere in that book did it say take in strangers suffering from mental illness."

He's right. The book was definitely more soup kitchen/ animal rescue type stuff. But isn't the idea the important part?

"Where's Allison?" he asks.

"I'm picking her up now."

"You're forbidden to take her home while that madman is in the house."

We stop arguing long enough to laugh at the idea of Roger forbidding me to do anything and then return to the subject at hand.

"He's not crazy," I say. "He's nice."

True, he eyed me like a juicy steak and said things that were inappropriate, but somehow I just know he's harmless. I'd bet my life on it.

"Would you have taken him home if he were ugly?" Roger asks. "If he had cold sores or a runny nose?"

"That's gross, Roger."

"Answer the question."

I don't want to answer because doing so will solidify my overall shallowness as a human being.

"I refuse," I say.

"Which means you would have left an ugly guy in the hospital. Hell, you would have left an ugly guy to have a meltdown in Target!"

I shrug. Roger can't see me.

"Whatever, honey," he says. "I think you're nuts, but who am I to say that what you're doing is wrong? Just make sure he's gone by bedtime."

I agree to his terms even if I'm not convinced I'm going to abide by them.

The moms gather in the tree-lined school quad, clucking like hens, waiting for the children to be released. I linger at the edge of the group, hoping I can avoid any conversations that end with invites to play tennis or have lunch at the club or do a 6:00 A.M. Bikram yoga class at the new place in town. "Hot yoga is so great for your pores!"

But sadly I seem to have forgotten my invisibility cloak at home. Belinda, my next-door neighbor, makes a beeline toward me. Her carefully maintained honey highlights are tied up in a neat ponytail. She wears expensive workout clothes that have yet to encounter a drop of sweat and a tight smile full of professionally bleached teeth. She is the kind of woman to whom you want to offer a sandwich. A human body requires more than four hundred calories a day to survive. Hell, I can knock back four hundred calories with one quick trip to Starbucks, but I'm just that kind of girl, I guess.

Belinda is on one end of the divorce continuum. Her mission in life is to replace her lost husband. She trolls Billsford for single men with the commitment of a Long Island bayman. I, who seek sex with no strings attached on Craigslist, occupy the other end. Conversation can be difficult.

"*Who* was the man in your minivan this afternoon?" Belinda demands with no preamble.

I experience a wave of queasiness. Belinda suffers from competitive man hunting. If she saw Cousin Harry, I'm sunk. No matter what I say, she will translate it to mean I have a gorgeous young lover, and within minutes the whole town will know.

"What?" I say. Playing dumb is always a great plan. Sometimes it even works.

"The. Hot. Man," she says, her face contorted in an unattractive way.

"There's no hot man," I say.

"Darling," she says, draping a skinny arm across my shoulders. "Are you suffering from memory loss?"

An icy finger of panic pokes me in the gut. I might be. There's half a chapter I have no memory of writing and a character I have no memory of creating.

"Well?" Belinda pushes.

"What?"

"The guy!" she shrieks. Several well-coiffed mom heads turn in our direction. I offer up a wan smile. Nothing strange happening over here. Nope.

"Sadie has a hot guy," Belinda announces. "And I mean, hot. Very hot. And young."

"You were using the binoculars, weren't you?" I ask.

Belinda gets out of answering as the moms swoop in. They come like zombies to brains, drawn by the words *hot, young,* and *guy.*

Where are the kids? They need to come out right now. They need to save me from the zombies.

"So?" Belinda says. I feel the eyes on me. They wait. They move closer. I start to hyperventilate.

"He's a second cousin once removed," I say finally. "He's visiting."

I stop before I give up too much of my story line. I don't want to be locked into details that don't work later on.

"That's it?" Belinda says.

"Sorry," I say. Oh please, release the children. As an alternative, a giant purple rhino charging through the quad would be acceptable.

"You need to put that guy in one of your books," Belinda sniffs. "He's devastating. That face. Wow."

Jesus, what sort of binoculars is she using these days? Military grade? But there is something in what she says that fills me with immediate dread, a close relation of panic but not exactly the same. I swallow hard. A sheen of sweat blooms on my forehead. What is it? What am I missing?

"So no details about your, ah, second cousin then?" Belinda asks with a wink.

"There aren't any," I say.

"Oh well, ladies," she says to the other moms, "I guess we'll have to wait for the book to get the dirty details."

I'm so terrified of the Billsford villagers storming my house with pitchforks and ostracizing my daughter for time infinitum that I still bang out one romance by Sadie Fuller every year to hide behind. It's what the neighbors think I do. But the Sadie Fuller romances are not what they once were. They're formulaic now, a chore. It's as clear as Lake Tahoe that my heart is elsewhere. Even my fans have begun to grumble. Soon K. T. Briggs and Sadie Fuller are going to have a smackdown, and I'm worried about how that will turn out.

"Not too dirty," I say. My voice sounds funny. I squeeze my hands into fists and push them into my thighs. Relax, goddamn it.

The moms drift away with an air of disappointment. No brains today. But Belinda stays put. She's like chewing gun in my hair.

"So," she says. "Do you want to do yoga with me tomorrow morning?"

The basis of my relationship with Belinda is purely geographical, as in she is my closest neighbor and obviously spies on me unapologetically. The only reason she doesn't know about Jason is that she's with her personal trainer doing squats on Friday mornings at 11:30. I understand Belinda is difficult to like and lonely, but I still don't want to do yoga with her.

"No," I say. "I work in the morning."

"Coffee?"

"I work all day, remember?"

"Early dinner?"

"I can't, Belinda," I say. "Oh look, here come the kids!"

Allison spills out of her fifth-grade classroom. She's surrounded as always by a gaggle of tall, skinny girls who look as if a strong breeze could blow them clean away. They wear clothes worse than anything I can conjure in my nightmares. There's a dress code at Holt, but they manage to work around it with tight, sparkly T-shirts, ridiculously short shorts, and sequined shoes. Some of them already wear makeup. Others have clearly mastered the porno pout. They have no idea what they are doing or why, but they feel its power. My heart aches every time I see them. Why rush into the adult mating game? There's a lifetime for it later. Besides, after a while, it's just chains wrapped around your ankles.

The girls chatter like squirrels, everyone speaking at once and no one listening. It's good practice for being a mother. You can talk all you want but it's very likely no one will hear you.

"Mommy," my not-so-little girl whispers as I hug her. I'm already living on borrowed time. Kissing in public has been a big no-go for at least a year and a half now.

"How was your day, honey?" We walk together, practically shoulder to shoulder. What is Greta putting in her meat loaf, Miracle-Gro? Just yesterday Allison was clinging to my knees at preschool.

"Good," Allison says. "We did science experiments and Rory got blue food coloring all over her face."

It pleases me to no end that I pay forty-five thousand dollars a year for my daughter to turn things blue with food coloring. As we head for home, I mull over the best way to present Cousin Harry the houseguest to Allison.

"So I have a friend over," I say as I drive. "You'll get to meet him when we get home."

But Allison doesn't hear me. She's plugged into her iPod. I worry about the next generation. How can you possibly have an original thought if you never experience silence? And when did *silence* become a dirty word? Maybe if I want to be really deviant in my next novel, I'll have the main character sit in absolute silence and do nothing. What a wild idea. Or maybe I'm just old.

"Allison!" I scream. I toss an empty paper coffee cup over the seat and hit her in the head.

"Mom," she says, annoyed. "What's *wrong* with you?"

I'm getting that a lot lately.

"I'm trying to talk to you," I say calmly. "Can you please remove your headphones?"

"Whatever," she mutters. I will not survive the teenage years. I will not. I will not.

"I said I have a friend visiting."

"Oh," Allison says. "Like he's hanging out with you?"

I occasionally get tripped up with the new meanings words have acquired over time. When I was young, hanging out did not involve fucking. It was sitting around someone's cheap apart-

ment or dorm room and smoking cigarettes. I choose to ignore the question to maintain my dignity.

"His name is Harry," I say. "I think you'll like him."

"Is he moving in?"

"No! Of course not. What gives you that idea?"

"Well, Jane's mother just invited the guy who teaches her golf at the club to move into their house. He's even sleeping in Jane's mother's room!"

That's because Jane's mother is a slut.

"Harry's just an old friend," I say. "We've never played golf together."

"Okay," Allison says. She seems done with this conversation. But it reminds me that I completely forgot to tell Greta about Harry before running off to get Allison. There's a good chance that by the time we get home, Harry will have been arrested for breaking and entering. Maybe I can spring him from a hospital and a prison all in one day? There has to be some sort of special do-gooder badge for that twofer.

"Can I listen to my music now?" Allison asks.

Whatever.

Chapter 13

When Allison and I finally get home, Greta greets us at the door with her thick arms crossed against her ample bosom. She glares at me like a spinster schoolmarm who's just discovered a stack of *Playgirl* magazines and an eighth of weed in her best student's locker. I'm in trouble.

"Hi," says Allison. She gives Greta a radiant smile and sweeps into the house, leaving me alone with the German tornado.

"Listen," I say. "Harry's an . . . old friend."

"Don't you mean second cousin once removed?" she says. When she's angry, her accent is much more intense. I cast my eyes down.

"I'm sorry I didn't give you any warning. But . . . well . . . I didn't have time and he's been ill and I thought I'd offer him our guest room while he recuperates."

"He looks healthy as a horse to me," Greta says, through tight lips.

"He's just a friend," I say for emphasis.

"He's very . . ." She pauses, searching for the right word.

"Good looking?" I offer.

"Yes. That's right. I'm not sure . . ."

"You've ever seen anything like him before?"

Greta gives me an annoyed look that says "stop finishing my sentences." I slip by her into the house.

Inside, Harry and Allison snack on toasts with goat cheese and fig jam, laid out on china plates, neatly folded linen napkins tucked alongside. Left to my own devices I'd feed my daughter Cheerios out of the box at every meal. But Greta has standards, and we are ever so grateful for them. They laugh about something, their heads together over the kitchen table.

Harry still wears his suit pants with the tear in the leg, but they are rolled up now to reveal well-muscled calves. His bare feet twitch and move under the table, dancing around like they're covered in ants, burning excess energy. I notice he has nice feet.

"Oh, for God's sake," I mutter.

"What's wrong, Mom?" Allison asks, still gazing at Cousin Harry with a dopey expression. I can read her thoughts: oh my god, oh my god. Oh. My. God.

"Nothing," I say. But really, who has nice feet? No one, that's who. Feet are inherently *not* nice. Toenails with yellow fungus, calluses, corns, cracks, blisters, bunions. Our feet bear the brunt of a great deal of abuse, and they look the part. I'll concede maybe newborn babies have cute feet, but that is only because they have not touched the ground yet. The minute they do, they are on the road to ugliness.

But Harry's feet are perfect. And Allison is already in love with him. Even Greta moves around the kitchen with her lips less pursed than usual.

"Ahem," I say.

Allison giggles. Harry pats her on the head like she's a puppy. She giggles again. I pull Harry out of his seat by the back of his shirt, not very gently.

"Harry and I have some work to do on the computer in my office," I say, pushing him ahead of me toward the stairs. He bounds up them like a panther, two at a time. I hurry along in his wake, a beat faster than normal. The effort leaves me breathless. Maybe I should throw myself on the sword and do that morning yoga class with nosy Belinda after all.

"Are we going to your bedroom?" Harry asks as we head down the hall.

"No!" I bark. "I said office."

"Just checking."

I stop short.

"Look," I say. "You and I, we're not going to have sex. Not now. Not later." You belong in the realm of fantasies. Reality would just ruin it.

"Really?" he asks.

"Really."

"No one has ever said that to me before." He's utterly perplexed.

"The only thing I want," I say, "is to figure out who you are and deliver you back to your people."

"Right," Harry says. "And I'm grateful." But I can tell the no-sex thing bothers him. It's clearly not something he's used to.

Just as I turn toward my office, a sharp, stabbing pain grips my chest. It's like the panic meter has been cranked up to an eleven. I gasp, leaning into the wall to keep from collapsing. I want to run, fast and away.

"Harry," I whisper. Cold sweat runs down my back.

Behind me, at the same moment, Harry falls to his knees, fighting for air as if he's being strangled. I sink down beside him. His pale face looms large, his eyes huge. Somehow the sight of him puts my own agony in perspective. If I drop dead in my own house, everyone will shake their heads and say I should have exercised more and laid off the mac and cheese. They'll be sad but not shocked. But if a virtual stranger dies in my house, I'm screwed. I have a horrible vision of burying Cousin Harry in the backyard under the rosebushes.

"Take a breath," I plead. "It's okay. Does your chest hurt? Tell me what's wrong."

He's fetal, his long, lithe body curled into a tight ball. The pain in my side is excruciating, like hundreds of tiny shards of glass are burrowing beneath my skin. I hold on to Harry's shoulder with one hand and dig the other into my side, praying the pressure will relieve some of the pain.

We are quite a pair.

"Say something," I demand. Harry's eyes flick to mine. He's terrified.

"Something's coming back," he says.

"It's okay," I say, pulling him into my lap as best I can. I stroke his hair like he's a baby. I wince.

Greta appears at the bottom of the stairs. She's too far away for me to read her face.

"Is everything all right?" she asks. "I heard a noise."

"Yes, yes," I say. I imagine, from her position, we probably appear as if we've moved on to our golf game. "Everything's fine. Harry just tripped. Right, Harry?"

I give him a nudge.

"Yes," he says. "I tripped." His voice catches. He closes his eyes.

"Tell me what you remember," I whisper. I can't take much more of this. The pain builds to a crescendo in my gut. I can't die. I have too much to do.

Silently, I berate myself for being stupid and impulsive and not taking seriously the potential cause of this man's memory loss. What if it's the result of some horrific trauma, like witnessing a murder or being forced to watch back-to-back episodes of *The Real Housewives of New Jersey*? What if he freaks out and goes berserk in my lovely house full of girls? I should *know* life is not controllable like a novel. Life is messy, and the plot never goes exactly as you'd like.

"My name is Aidan Hathaway," he says.

And just like that, the pain vanishes.

Chapter 14

There are rules for almost every professional pursuit, and that's no different for fiction writing. If you write mysteries, you better have your facts straight. If you write humor, you'd better not be annoying your readers by chapter three. After my first K. T. Briggs book came out, I received a letter from a helpful fan named Ellen. The letter started out "Dear Hack" and just got better from there.

Ellen was furious she had given me several hours of her life that she would never get back and I had betrayed her trust. I had broken the rules. There is a covenant between reader and writer, and I'd stomped all over it.

Ellen did not fall in love with my romantic hero. She did not identify with the heroine. She was appalled there was sex before the midpoint in the novel, and she thought my strategically placed coincidences were ridiculous.

"You can't blame it all on the evil twin," she wrote. "Who does that?"

By this point in the letter, I was feeling pretty bad about myself, but I plowed on. Ellen's next complaint was that I used, or overused in her opinion, plot at the expense of conflict.

"There can't be makeup sex without conflict," she moaned. "You're so wrapped up in what they're doing, you ignore how they're *feeling.*" I thought this was interesting. To this day, I'm not totally sure I understand what she meant, but I give her credit for trying.

Quickly, she moved on to the issue of secondary characters. I had too many. Naturally.

"They take up so much time!" she hollered from the page. "I hate them!"

Ellen was also kind enough to point out that my "I only have eyes for you" was lacking and that my "happily ever after" was not convincing enough. She had doubts about the future of my hero and heroine. Was a sequel planned? A trilogy? Was that my reason? She found she could not sleep on account of worrying for them. In fact, she was writing this letter at 2:00 A.M.

But fear not. At the end of the letter, Ellen grudgingly complimented my use of dialogue, which I thought was big of her.

I appreciate all fan mail, despite its actual content. It's flattering to have a person I do not know take even a minute out of her busy life to make contact with me. I read and respond to

each e-mail, every letter, and sometimes I even tweet, although when I tell Allison that she rolls her eyes. I cannot possibly understand social media. I am simply too old.

So there I sat with Ellen's old-fashioned letter in my hands, wondering how best to respond to her, when I had a thought. Maybe Ellen was onto something. Maybe I was working outside the boundaries when I'd be better off staying within them.

I pulled out a piece of paper and grabbed a thick, black Sharpie. I would cull Ellen's letter down into a list. Across the top I scrawled "The Rules." When I was done, I pinned the list to the big, messy bulletin board above my desk, where I would have no choice but to see it every time I sat down.

It has been there ever since. And nowhere on that list is it mentioned that romantic heroes can reality-bend and turn up in the author's house. It just doesn't happen. If you don't believe me, ask Ellen.

"What the hell are you talking about?" I say to Cousin Harry after a moment of stunned silence. I shove him off my lap and slide away until I bump into a pretty little table holding a pretty little lamp. I catch the lamp midair. Mere hours ago, I was here in this hallway with Jason, my head pounding against the wall. Perhaps all that pounding gave me a concussion and I'm hallucinating, because I think Cousin Harry just identified himself as the hero from *Stolen Secrets*.

Which no one has read yet.

"My name is Aidan Hathaway," he says again in a rush. "I live at Fifty Central Park South. I have a collection of antique roadsters I keep in a warehouse in Brooklyn. There's a small Van Gogh in my bathroom. My bedroom is white except for one wall which is a window looking out on the park. I'm the Chairman and CEO of Hathaway Enterprises. I'm twenty-nine years old."

My ears ring.

"Please be quiet," I say.

"Oh my God," he says, grinding the heels of his palms into his temples. "It's like a flood. I have a driver named Thomas, and my father is dead."

He continues to rattle off bits and pieces about his rarefied existence. There is no way this man could have seen my outline and character summaries for *Stolen Secrets*, and yet most everything he says of Aidan Hathaway is true. I know this because I wrote it.

"You're out of your mind," I say. "How did you read the book? Tell me."

At my last Romance Writers of America conference, an author friend of mine, now solidly A list, told me she knew she'd arrived on the shores of success when she had her first stalker. It turned out to be a young woman with bad acne and a lot of time on her hands, but still, it was significant. Is Harry my stalker? If so, it's a hell of an elaborate plot he's concocted to get inside my house. I'd be flattered if the idea were not so inherently terrifying.

"What book?" Harry asks. He looks genuinely confused, but I'm not buying it.

"My book!" I shriek. He leans away from me.

"I thought you wanted to know who I was," he says. "This should make you happy."

I cannot scream at him in the hallway. I have Allison and Greta to consider, so I stand up, grab him by the back of his T-shirt, and haul him to his feet. He protests, but I don't care. I shove him inside my office and slam the door before either of us can escape. I still hold him by the shirt when, for perhaps the first time all day, I *really* look at him. And just like that, my world blurs at the edges, as if the walls are closing in. I take an involuntary step back.

His eyes are green and wide set. They are the same eyes as those of a boy I loved in college. That boy died in a car accident on a country road in Connecticut, but I put a piece of him in every one of my heroes, a tribute of sorts to what might have been. Big hands grip the arms of my desk chair, where I have planted him. They're the hands of a German butcher Greta favors. From time to time, I pick things up at his shop, and he always wipes those meaty hands on his white apron before handing me the packages, bound up in brown paper. I love those hands.

His flawless pale skin, now slightly red from stress and exertion, comes directly from a young man I saw several times, randomly, over the course of a single snowy week in December. He popped up at the grocery store, at the bookstore, and once on the southbound train platform. After that I never saw him again, but his marble skin made an impression on me.

The dark hair, a little long and curling ever so slightly at the ends, belongs to the guy who bags my groceries at Whole Foods. He's so hip it almost hurts, but his hair is close to perfect. Every time I see him, I want to run my hands through it.

Trembling, I reach out and push that same fabulous hair from my stranger's forehead. Starting at the outermost edge of his right eyebrow and running up about two inches, is a thin, faint scar.

"How did you get this?" I whisper.

"I crashed the vintage 1971 Porsche 917/10 Spyder Can-Am when I was thirteen," he says, his voice so low I can barely make out the words. "I crashed it into an old oak tree on Dad's estate. The tree died and Dad never forgave me."

Backstory is a funny thing. It can make its way to paper or stay tucked away in a writer's head, buried in the gray matter under shopping lists and bra sizes. In this case, I planned to unveil the background of the scar later on in *Stolen Secrets*. Yes, our stunning young man had to be rich, beautiful, and broody, but if I could show my readers he was raised by unloving wolves, they would ultimately see his vulnerability and fall in love with him. And the readers *must* fall in love with him, as Ellen had suggested. Those are the rules.

In this case, the details of the scar, which occurred to me while driving past a huge oak that, every fall, turns a spectacular orange, never made it to paper. They lived in my head.

I can take this apart a thousand different ways, but the fact remains that the man sitting in front of me is the perfect physical manifestation of Aidan Hathaway. Without another word,

I pick up the paper recycling bin and puke bits of fig and goat cheese into it.

"Jesus, Sadie," Aidan Hathaway says. "That's disgusting."

Still holding the bin, I back away from him until I'm flat against the wall. I slide down to the bamboo floor.

"Are you ill? Were the figs contaminated?"

I hold up a hand for him to stop. Please just stop talking.

"Don't move," I say. My voice is oddly distorted. But I seem to get my point across because Aidan does not get up and run away. He sits very still, his eyes bouncing from me to the puke.

Pushing the bin in front of me, I crawl on all fours out of the office. If I stand up, there is a good chance I will pass out. Finally, I make it to the bathroom. I stow the recycle bin in the shower and pull the curtain to hide the evidence. I splash cold water on my face, which appears red and blotchy in the mirror's reflection. My eyes are dilated. I look like your garden-variety crackhead.

"You're not crazy, Sadie," I tell myself. "It's all just some big misunderstanding."

I've gotten away with some outlandish plot twists in my day, but even I'm not buying the misunderstanding bit. I dry my face, take a big swig of Listerine, and creep back to my office. I peer inside. Aidan sits with his perfect feet up on my desk and his hands clasped behind his head. If I were to lean back in my desk chair that far, I'd end up on my ass, but he looks comfortable.

Strange things happen in life. What's important is how we

deal with them. Or at least that's what Greta always says. I step into the room. Aidan spins toward me.

"Do you know a woman named Clarissa?" I demand.

"No," he says quickly. But his expression is one of puzzlement, as if the wisp of a memory floated by, much too thin to grab.

"Are you sure?" I push.

"I . . . I don't know," he says. "No. I don't think so."

I lunge for the Xanax on the desk behind him. I'm over my limit, but sometimes more is better. So what if I fall asleep on my feet?

"It's very important," I say, "for you to tell me the last thing you remember."

He closes his eyes and concentrates.

"It's vague," he says. "I remember a flash of light and pain in my leg. And I was with . . . Lily."

"And?"

"And this Clarissa person showed up! This awful woman!"

He jumps out of the chair, hands clenched into fists. A vein throbs in his neck.

"Lily just vanished. Into thin air," he says, grabbing me by the shoulders. I stagger backward. "And then Clarissa said the only way I could save Lily was to go after her. She offered me a deal."

"The deal she gave you was forty-eight hours to find your ladylove, uncover the magic spell, and get back," I add.

Aidan stops short.

"How do you know?" he asks.

I remember the first time I read Hemingway and how I marveled at his exquisite economy of words. It's hard for me to get away with that style when mostly I'm searching for new ways to describe basic fornication. But I give it a go now.

"I wrote you," I say. I gesture to the laptop as if that will somehow explain my bizarre statement.

"Wrote me?" he says. "Like a letter or an e-mail?"

Then again, sometimes an economy of words leads to confusion. I tell him about how after his father's funeral, he drank the Macallan 1926 in his bathroom all alone and cried. I tell him about Lily's shirt and the lipstick in the elevator. I tell him about how they locked eyes in the hallway at the reception for the new champagne.

Aidan has gone so white, I can almost see through him.

Chapter 15

Aidan and I sit in my office. He breathes erratically, a prelude to hyperventilation. The heat from the day pushes in on us despite the drawn curtains. We have finished reading the first three, and only, chapters of *Stolen Secrets*.

"I don't understand," Aidan says flatly.

"Me neither," I say.

"How could you have let that crazy lady follow us?" Aidan asks. He has plot issues, which I can understand, but somehow I feel he's missing the larger point here.

"I didn't write that part," I say.

"But you said this was your book, so you either wrote it or you didn't write it," Aidan fumes. "You can't have it both ways. This is turning out to be a very bad day."

"Listen," I say. "I wrote the beginning of that third chapter, but I didn't write the end."

"So who did?"

"I think Clarissa did." I can't believe I said that out loud.

"But who the hell is Clarissa?" Aidan yells. His fury creates more heat than this tiny room can possibly hold. I'm in a full sweat. "And why is she fucking with me?"

I have no idea. There is no Clarissa in his backstory.

But before I can lay that unsatisfying answer on him, Greta appears in the doorway. She wears a neutral expression and says nothing, just focuses on furious Aidan. If she's scared for me and ready to call for help, she shows no sign of it.

"Greta?"

She clears her throat.

"You have the Holt fund-raiser in ninety minutes," she says after a long silence. "Your dress is in the closet, and I took the liberty of dusting off the appropriate shoes."

There's something about the mention of the fund-raiser, an ordinary event in what I used to consider an ordinary world, that leaves me feeling stunned. Greta interprets this to mean I'm lurching around for an excuse not to attend in favor of staying home and playing footsie with the man I kidnapped from the hospital. And there is no way she will stand by for that sort of shirking of one's duties.

"You're part of the organizing committee," she reminds me. "You have three minutes at the microphone at exactly nine

o'clock to encourage people to donate large sums of money to the school. During dessert and coffee."

Goddamn it.

"I really thought tuition was going to be it," I say, almost to myself.

"But it's not," Greta answers. "It's never as you think." For a split second, I wonder if we are talking about the same thing. Greta plants her hands on her big hips and fills the doorway. She won't shove off until she sees some action on my part.

"Right," I say. "I'll go get dressed."

Greta gives me a curt nod and leaves. Aidan rests his forehead on my desk. His body shakes all over, and I can't tell if it is because his anger has turned to fear.

"Keep it together," I say. "We'll make a plan. We'll figure out what to do."

"We're all going to die," he says matter-of-factly.

This is not something I would ever have him say. It shows weakness, vulnerability, and possibly, good common sense, none of which is an acceptable emotion in an erotic male lead.

"Oh, for God's sake, Aidan, snap out of it!" I say. It takes me just a moment to realize I have called him Aidan as opposed to Harry. I have gone down the rabbit hole. I push on.

"What would Lily think to see you like this? Be brave."

He reacts as if I've just slapped him across the face. His eyes go cold and dark with some inner turmoil. He clenches his fists, releases them, just as he was doing in Target earlier.

He seems capable of violence, but so do most men if backed into a corner.

"We'll find Lily," I say again, slowly, calmly. "We'll deal with this." He begins to relax.

"You're right," he says. "We will. I'm overreacting."

Well, not really, but why mince words?

Aidan follows me to my bedroom and sits on the bed as I paw through my drawers looking for a full-length Spanx suit that will compress me enough so I can fit into my dress but not so much that I pass out from lack of oxygen. It's a fine line, and I'm already sweating.

As Aidan makes himself perfectly comfortable on my bed, he spins scenarios about who Clarissa might be, one more preposterous than the next, until he gets a glimpse of the Spanx. I always say there's nothing like your first encounter with Spanx to get your mind off your troubles.

"Is that something you wear?" he asks in disbelief.

"It's a compression garment," I say, as if that explains all. I guess I'd be more mortified if we hadn't already broken ground with the skort exchange earlier. "What're you doing in here anyway?"

"Thinking out loud. Waiting for you to tell me the plan." He takes the Spanx from me. He pulls it end to end. "If I was banished last night, does that mean we only have twenty-four hours to find Lily and get out of here? Or did the clock start when you found me this morning in that store? In either case, it's not a lot of time."

This is perhaps one of the stranger conversations I've had in

my bedroom. Aidan stretches the Spanx very thin and tries to look through it. It covers his face, like the updated version of the hockey-mask-wearing psycho killer.

"Stop that right now," I say. "And I'm aware of the time. Really. But I have to show up at the fund-raiser tonight." Sadie Fuller, mom, does not blow off obligatory school functions, as appealing as the idea often is.

He throws the Spanx aside, puts his hands behind his head, and settles down on my pillows to wait for me to tell him what is going to happen next. The muscles in his arms bulge, and I swear he's flexing them for my benefit.

He looks good lying on my bed. He looks male and young and alive. I gather my Spanx and my not-so-little black dress and head into the bathroom, thinking I might still have time to drown myself in the toilet before things get much worse.

"Can I come with you?" Aidan shouts through the closed door.

What? Are you mad? Out in public? I'd be torn to shreds on the school quad come Monday morning. Inside the bathroom, I struggle into the Spanx, panting from the exertion. I pull and push and rearrange my flesh under the skintight garment, striving for a smooth surface. I push my gigantic breasts up so they spill fetchingly, I hope, over the top of the bodice. It's so hot. The Spanx makes it worse. This must be what it feels like to be a St. Bernard living in Boca Raton.

"It might be a good place to gather clues about where to find Lily," Aidan adds.

"That's ridiculous," I say flatly. I hear him in my bedroom rummaging through the junk on my night table. I pull on my dress, struggling with the zipper as single women do. "Plus, I don't do mysteries."

"I think you do now," he says. And he does have a point. Recent events register pretty high on the mysterious scale. They also register pretty high on the "are you out of your mind?" scale, but there seems little point in traveling that road.

I open the bathroom door.

"Well?" Aidan asks. "Am I in?"

I think about him working the crowd. Belinda, the moms from school, a handful of bored fathers, Roger and Fred, or the man who has already replaced Fred. My gay ex-husband always brings a date to these events. I never do. We laugh about it. Or Roger does. I feel bad about myself, but I can't admit that to Roger because it would hurt his feelings. So what if I show up with the gorgeous, young, virile babe lying on my bed right now? What happens if *that* happens?

I put my mascara down. I can't actually be considering this. But he does have a really nice suit. Sure, there's a tear in the leg, but we can fix that easily enough. I stare at my reflection in the mirror. There are plenty of lines now where there used to be smooth skin and spots that no amount of expensive fading serums can banish. My lips are less full than they once were, and I feel dishonest blaming the bags under my eyes on poor sleep. They are part of my face now, pulling everything else down with them. But age happens only if you are lucky, so I try to go easy

on my face and body. They are doing the best they can with the materials at hand.

My mind, however, is another topic completely. It has always been tight as a wire and flexible as a Cirque du Soleil performer. It is my crown jewel even if I generally keep that to myself. But now there is a fictional character sitting on my bed, expressing a desire to attend a Holt Hall fund-raiser as my date. Nobody wants to go to a fund-raiser unless they have to, so right there, things are not as they should be.

Let's look at the specifics. First, the man on my bed does not exist solely in my head because a dozen other people have seen him. He was examined by a doctor, and last time I checked, doctors don't examine mental hallucinations. Second, the possibility of it being an elaborate hoax seems remote. There are too many details, like the scar, that no one but me knows. Third, he's total eye candy. I should bring him to the fund-raiser. I mean, if I'm having a nervous breakdown, I might as well enjoy the ride, right?

"Sadie," I tell myself. "You're an idiot."

"What?" Aidan calls from the bedroom.

"Nothing," I say.

"So? Can I come?"

Downstairs I announce that Cousin Harry likes to go by his middle name, Aidan, and that's what we should call him. But Allison doesn't care if we call him late for dinner; she's just pissed I'm not leaving him here for her to play with.

"I wanted him to watch *Glee* with me," she says. "I recorded it!"

"Greta will be here," I say.

"She hates *Glee*," Allison says. "She thinks it's silly and unrealistic. That's what she said."

"Then pick something else to watch," I say. "*Dancing with the Stars*? Greta likes that one."

There's intense pouting from my daughter. She scowls at me. But before she can move on to something louder and more dramatic, Aidan appears. We both stare, jaws dropped.

"Will this work?" he asks with a wink. His hair is tousled just so, his face clean shaven and smooth. The hole in his pant leg has been expertly mended, and the suit and shirt both pressed into tip-top shape. I see Greta's handiwork behind the mending and the pressing. The idea of inhabiting the same house as a wrinkly or otherwise compromised garment, even briefly, is offensive to her. Aidan's fingers play with the knot in his tie, nestled at his throat.

"You look nice," Allison stammers.

Even his shoes are buffed to a shine.

"Yeah," I say.

From behind his back, Aidan produces a single blooming rose, plucked from the backyard garden.

"For you," he says with a slight bow. "You look very beautiful."

Allison blushes on my behalf. I take the rose and hand it to her. She scampers away, her nose buried in the silky petals.

"Thank you," I say. But I don't believe the line about being beautiful, because how beautiful can I look when I'm slowly asphyxiating in my dress? And I have real concerns about what

will happen when I try to sit down. Exactly how much pressure can be brought to bear on your average zipper anyway?

"Bye, Allison," I shout. "Good-bye, Greta."

No one answers me, so I head out the door on the arm of my fabulously gorgeous, twenty-nine-year-old stud.

Chapter 16

Aidan is quiet as we drive toward the Lake House Restaurant, which is neither by a lake nor in a house. It's in a strip mall, with all the charm that implies. As Aidan looks out the window into the fading light of the day, I wonder what he could possibly be thinking. I touch him on the leg. He startles.

"Hey," I say. "How are you?"

He sighs. It's long and drawn out so I'm sure not to miss it.

"I miss Lily," he says.

How can you miss someone you barely know? I mean, they only had a couple of chapters together. And I don't care how good the author is, a couple of chapters does not make a relationship.

"But you two weren't exactly an item," I point out.

He turns toward me, pulling aside the shoulder harness of the seat belt so he can get a better angle.

"No," he says. "But I felt like I knew her. She struck me like a hammer when I first saw her at that marketing reception. I hadn't intended to go, but fate intervened. And then I made sure she was given the Hathaway account so I could see her again."

"Wow," I say. "That's interesting." But really, you don't have to tell me this. This part I already know.

"I just knew it was something special," he continues, warming to his topic. "Lily and I, we connect. My best friend, Erin, always says that love will find a way in. It may be tricky and it may surprise you, but it will find a way. And it turns out she is exactly right."

"You have a best friend named Erin?" I ask.

"Yes. So?"

I grip the steering wheel a little harder. There's no best friend named Erin. But then again, there was no witch named Clarissa either.

"Right," I say. "Your best friend, Erin. She has a way with words."

"You've never had this happen," Aidan says bluntly. He pulls at a long strand of hair and twirls it around his finger, just as he did in Target.

"If you keep doing that, you're going to end up with a bald spot," I say. He looks aghast but releases the hair. He regroups.

"So?" he asks.

"Are you talking about love at first sight? Soul mates? No thank you. Those are just dangerous ideas that build expectations. Unreasonable expectations."

"No, Sadie," he says. "They're magical words." He sounds moony, dopey. It doesn't at all fit what he is supposed to be. "I felt so awake all of a sudden when I met Lily. But it was like I didn't know I was sleeping. Magical."

"You said that already," I say.

"I don't think you can understand until it happens to you," he says dismissively.

"I guess."

I can't believe I'm wearing a fancy dress, driving a minivan, and discussing true love with a man I made up. I couldn't get anyone to take those odds, even in Vegas.

"So Lily," I say.

"Lily. My God," Aidan says, smashing the dashboard with a closed fist and making me jump in the driver's seat. "She must be terrified. I should be out there looking for her right now!"

The way Aidan moves seamlessly from calm and serene to dramatically emotive is remarkable. I've written more finely nuanced characters in my time.

"The New York metropolitan area has almost twenty million people," I say. "You ever hear the one about the needle in a haystack? But in the dark this time. No. We need to think about where exactly to look for her."

"She's a delicate flower," Aidan says. Did he even hear me? "So fragile, so gentle, so trusting and giving."

"Stop that right now," I command.

He shuts his mouth.

"So?"

"So what?"

"Any ideas?"

"Not one," he says.

Not helpful.

"Well, it wouldn't make sense for Clarissa to drop you both in the same place," I say. "She wants to make the task of finding Lily almost impossible, right? She wants to enjoy the show while you stumble around in the dark and ultimately fail." I feel like I'm running lines for a low-budget paranormal cable TV show. It causes me some pain.

"The way you put it, Sadie, it sounds like I'm on a quest."

Books with quests do really well. Especially young adult. Maybe if I wrote more quests I'd be sitting here with a half-god, half-mortal ten-year-old armed with clairvoyance and the ability to explain to me just what the hell is going on. That would be easier in some ways.

"Clarissa dropped you in a totally foreign place," I say. "A place where you would have difficulty orienting yourself. Just as she said she would in the manuscript."

"That horrible store with the horrible lighting." Aidan shudders at the memory of Target.

"And she said she was sending Lily to a dark New York City," I say. "A place she'd be alone. Does that mean anything to you?"

"Not really. You can see New York City from the moon."

He's right of course. New York is as bright as a Christmas tree star. Even the dark bars and empty alleys are bathed in ambient light. But now we have step one of our plan.

"We need to think of dark places in New York where Clarissa could have sent Lily, where she'd be alone. We need a list."

Aidan nods his head. "Yes," he says. "A list. Great."

"By the time we leave the dinner tonight, I want you to have five things on your list. Five places we can look for Lily. Got it?"

"You're bossy," Aidan says. It's more an observation than a criticism. I remind myself erotic heroes rarely encounter women like me.

"You don't know the half of it," I say.

We pull into the restaurant parking lot. My fellow fund-raisers are visible through the large plate-glass windows. They hold glasses of wine and wear unnatural, tight smiles. I glance at Aidan. This is a bad idea. A man like Aidan requires an explanation, and the truth is simply not an option.

"Oh, and if anyone asks," I say, gingerly climbing out of the minivan, trying not to burst my dress, "you're my second cousin once removed."

"Huh?" He manages his exit gracefully, but then again, he's not asphyxiating.

"The people here are going to want to know who you are and why you're with me. Plus I told the quad moms that you were visiting, so just go with it, okay?"

"What's a quad mom?" he asks.

"Nothing to be afraid of," I say. "They usually don't bite."

I've never been one to make an entrance. When I come into a room, people do not pause midconversation to collectively acknowledge my fabulousness. They go on talking or laughing or drinking or eating finger food or whatever, and that's fine. I'm happy sliding in at the edges, circling cautiously until I find the place in the crowd where I might best fit. At most school functions, I behave like bad sex: I'm in and I'm out and I'm done.

But lurking on the sidelines and pretending I'm invisible won't work tonight, as my "date" is the human equivalent of a disco ball. Aidan extends me his elbow, I take it, and we walk into the crowded restaurant, already abuzz with cocktails and gossip. As we cross the threshold, a complete and total silence engulfs the room. I can hear the background music clearly, some pop country stuff that will get stuck in my head and stay there forever.

The silence lasts for three seconds, which is an eternity if you think about it. All eyes are on Aidan. The women lick their lips and the men instinctively flex their biceps. The whole scene is completely absurd. The president of the PTA, a taut, fit woman named Felicity, glides up to me on strappy silver heels.

"Sadie," she purrs. "So *nice* to see you. Who's your *friend?*" She flashes her remarkably white teeth in my direction, but her eyes remain on Aidan. I know what she's thinking. This man is above my pay grade, a fancy accessory I cannot possibly afford.

"Aidan Hathaway," I say. "This is Felicity Harrington." Felicity cocks her head coyly to one side and extends a manicured hand in his direction.

"My pleasure," she says. And she really means it.

Aidan takes Felicity's hand in both of his and stares deep into her eyes. Her shoulders go limp, her posture collapses, and she lets go with a guttural sigh, which is probably more noise than she made the last time she and her husband, Chip the investment banker, had sex. And that could have been five years ago. You never can tell around here. I tap her shoulder to bring her back to reality.

"Oh my," she says, still not looking at me.

"Yeah," I say, taking Aidan by the arm and steering him toward the bar.

"Nice to meet you!" Felicity calls out after us.

"Don't do that again," I whisper to Aidan.

"Do what?"

"Put the girls in a trance or whatever it is you do," I say.

"I was just being friendly," he says.

"Well, be less friendly then. I don't want them following us home like cats in heat."

"You have a lot of rules."

"Rules are important," I say.

But that's only part of the problem. The other part is that in the flesh, Aidan has many more dimensions than he does on the page. For example, I describe certain attributes and you, the reader, fill in the rest. Maybe in your head Aidan Hathaway looks like a young Pierce Brosnan or that guy in college who would never give you the time of day. Whatever it is, the image belongs to you and you alone. Now, with the man standing before me, I see how his nose is slightly off center or how his lopsided smile makes him less intimidating. I never mentioned those things. I never thought them. Aidan is expanding to fill his own space. To be honest, it's throwing me off balance, which considering where I started, is dangerous territory indeed.

The bartender, an attractive gay man from a local restaurant, flirts openly with Aidan, and Aidan flirts back. My drink is so strong I almost spit it out. When was the last time I got a heavy pour at a fund-raising event? I'll tell you. Never. Good looking gets a stiff drink; middle aged gets a pitying smile.

I'm enjoying the wallop of the drink when Roger appears at my side. He's dressed to kill, in a dark suit and a bright blue tie. He tries to pinch my ass, but that's a no-go on account of the Spanx.

"Good lord, Sadie, can you breathe?" he asks.

"Only a little," I admit.

"Honey, I don't understand why you do it," he says, shaking his head.

"Because otherwise I would have to come to these things in my pajamas," I say. "And that would be embarrassing. Is that Fred?"

Roger rolls his eyes. The resemblance to his eleven-year-old daughter is striking.

"Yes," he whispers, "but before you go off, I did not want to come to this thing alone, and if I dumped Fred last night after I talked to you, even I would not have had time to round up another suitable date."

"Oh, I don't know, Roger. You might have pulled it off."

He laughs because he kind of knows I'm right, but the sound

evaporates when Aidan turns his attention from the bartender back to us.

"Aidan Hathaway," I announce. Aidan flashes one of his knee-bending smiles. "I'd like you to meet Allison's father, Roger Evanston."

"I thought you said his name was Harry," Roger whispers.

"I was wrong," I say. Really wrong.

Suddenly, Fred appears.

"Oh my," he gasps. "I'm Fred. *Who* are you?"

Everyone shakes hands. There is grinning and slobbering and fawning, and Fred whisks Aidan away in search of the cheese display. Roger stares after them.

"Is that really the hospital guy?" he asks, unable to hide his astonishment.

Affirmative.

"Well, no wonder you brought him home."

"Yeah," I say. I take a big swig of my toxic gin and tonic. It's wonderful.

"So are you, you know, taking advantage of him?" Roger asks. I'm very liberal. In fact, in a town like Billsford, I'm so far to the left I've almost disappeared over the edge. But I'm still not comfortable discussing my sex life with my gay ex-husband. He knows nothing about Jason, and that's the way I plan to keep it. I couldn't stomach the scrutiny.

"No," I sniff. "I'm old enough to be his mother. It's gross." Plus Aidan is packed full of sharp, hard muscles. I might hurt myself on one of his angles.

"I guess you're right," Roger says finally. "Ashton did end up dumping Demi in the end."

I agree, as if the foibles of the rich and deranged have any bearing on my life. We watch Aidan sharing cheese with Fred. Although he promised he would stop, Aidan has clearly put Fred in a trance.

"So?" Roger asks.

"What?"

"How's Allison?"

"Great. You're still taking her tomorrow night?"

"Of course," he says. "I promised her a shopping expedition."

The translation of that statement is: Please send her with your credit card. Fred and Aidan reappear. Fred whispers in Roger's ear, and they excuse themselves. I have no doubt they are headed for a stall in the men's room or Fred's car in the parking lot.

"Fred asked me if I ever thought I might be gay," Aidan says, a sly smile on his face. "I think I disappointed him when I told him no."

"Fred's a bit of an optimist," I said.

"So how did you end up married to a man who doesn't like women?"

Oh, if I had a dollar for every time someone asked me that question, I'd be kicking back poolside in Aruba right now.

"Roger likes women," I sniff. "Just not in that way."

"You know what I mean."

Aruba, fix me an umbrella drink! Here I come!

"He hadn't come to terms with being gay when we got married," I say. Plus I was knocked up. Oddly, admitting I married a man who loves musicals and rom-coms with Jennifer Aniston and can discuss what shade of green to paint the bedroom for hours on end is easier than saying I got pregnant when I wasn't paying attention. I wish I understood why that is the case.

"We're still good friends," I say. "And both very involved in Allison's life."

Well, I do all the heavy lifting, but why quibble over details? I don't want to talk about this anymore. It's killing my buzz.

"How's your list going?" I ask.

"I think I'd do better with another drink," Aidan says. "To the bar? Shall we mingle along the way? Work the crowd a bit?"

He holds his arm out to me, and I take it. If he's concerned about his one true love being stranded in some godforsaken place all alone, he's doing a good job hiding it.

Chapter 17

Aidan and I move slowly around the room. Everyone wants to talk to us. Aidan gets invited on seven golf outings and I to four country club lunches that I will skip as my threshold for torture is not quite that high. Everyone talks about the heat wave, the need to support Holt Hall's endowment, and how fantastic Aidan must look naked. I exaggerate, yes, but I know what they're thinking. We secure more drinks and snack on sushi and fresh spring rolls.

Aidan feeds me a cold shrimp dripping with cocktail sauce as if it were the most natural thing in the world. It's oddly erotic, but perhaps that's my two stiff gin and tonics talking. I make a concerted effort to lock my knees. Having them buckle here will not help my reputation. I'm already at risk of waking up not as

"Allison's mom, the writer" but as "the divorced lady with the delicious young lover."

That we are not actually lovers is beside the point. Every single person in this room assumes I'm having sex with Aidan Hathaway. The women are thinking I must have taken those postbirth Kegel exercises seriously to land such a perfect specimen, and the men are wishing they could *be* Aidan Hathaway just for an afternoon. Of course, they would immediately dump their forty-something wives and make a beeline for the nearest anorexic Brazilian model, but that is to be expected. Pop culture almost demands it.

I stop thinking about Brazilian models long enough to realize Aidan is gone. I scan the room. Off to one side, along a wall, long tables have been uncovered to reveal silent auction items. Felicity has her arm linked through Aidan's, giving him a personal tour of what's available. I fully expect her to hop up there and add herself to the auction booty. Aidan waves me over.

"I'd like to buy something to support Allison," he says. "Felicity here suggested the rare champagne collection. What do you think about that?"

I glance at the suggested bid, which is three thousand dollars.

"It's a lovely thought," I whisper to him. "But you can't. You have no money." And as much as I enjoy a chilled glass of bubbly, four bottles at that price feels a bit steep. Let the investment bankers have at it.

"What are you talking about?" Aidan asks. "I have billions.

Really, Sadie, I'm very rich. I have a warehouse full of vintage sports cars and a penthouse."

"Not here."

Aidan instinctively goes for his wallet, to prove his point. I shake my head.

"You have the clothes you came through with," I say quietly. "And probably you should be grateful for that."

But I give him credit. While he mentally reorganizes the known universe and his place in it, his face remains neutral.

"Nothing?"

"No," I say.

"I can't even afford a bottle of champagne?"

No. The auction does not accept alternative reality Visa or MasterCard. I shake my head again.

A tap on my shoulder interrupts our discussion of fiscal solvency. I turn to find my neighbor Belinda wearing a skintight getup designed to highlight her long hours in the gym, and her date, Jason. My Jason. More specifically, my Friday late morning Jason. This does not help my equilibrium.

"Hello there," Belinda says, scanning Aidan head to toe, as if figuring how she can stuff him in her tiny clutch and dash off to Hedonism II for a spell of nakedness. "This is my *date*. Jason Blair. Jason is an *attorney* in New York. For a *big* firm."

How on earth do we play this? We can't very well confess we met a while back when we were both trolling for sex on Craigslist. This is Billsford. They would ask us to leave. I wait for Jason to say something, but his eyes are locked on Aidan.

"Hi," I say too loudly. I stick out my hand. "Nice to meet you."

Jason takes it, but he can't stop looking at Aidan.

"This is Aidan Hathaway," I say. All night, I've introduced him as my second cousin once removed, but not now. His name hangs in the air.

I wait to equalize, for the rational part of my brain to remind me that Jason and I use each other only for sex. There is no commitment or relationship beyond Friday mornings, thus making any level of jealousy inappropriate.

Belinda likes Aidan even better up close. She quizzes him about how he's enjoying the food because, of course, she has yet to take a bite. She tells Aidan she lives next door. She does not mention the binoculars. Aidan tells her he's staying with me for a bit and maybe they can wave hello to each other. He winks. She quivers. Jason grinds his teeth, the muscles in his jaw jutting out. I remain off balance.

"We should go," I say to Aidan. "Allison's at home watching *Dancing with the Stars*. That can be dangerous after a while."

It's a lie. Allison is fine, but the wind has gone out of my fun sails. I now have an image of naked Jason and naked Belinda, naked together, to keep me company, and it is making me queasy. Or maybe it's the heat, the alcohol, and the Spanx.

"We can't leave just yet," Aidan says. He throws a big smile at Belinda, who clutches Jason's arm to keep from being knocked over by pure radiance. "You've got three minutes at the microphone in . . ." He glances at his watch. "Well, look at that! Right now."

Before I can protest, Aidan takes me under a sweaty armpit and tosses me right into the loving embrace of Headmis-
tress Leticia Woolworth, who stands very erect by the buffet
table, clutching the cordless microphone. Aidan greets her with
a slight bow. She lowers her eyes demurely and extends a hand.
Blue bloods recognize blue bloods. It's like they can smell each
other, the musty whiff of eau d'Mayflower.

"Such a pleasure to meet you, Mr. Hathaway," she says with
a coy smile. "I'm always so happy when our single parents find
love again, especially with our kind of people." She winks. My
jaw literally drops in horror.

"Sadie's quite a woman," Aidan says. I can see the gears turning in his head. There's an opening and he's taking it. He slides
an arm around my waist and pulls me toward him as if I am
a much less ravishing Scarlett O'Hara. The motion throws my
head back, so I have no hope of avoiding his luscious lips as they
lock onto mine.

I see stars and stripes and glitter. Or maybe the restaurant
has an American flag painted on the ceiling? Aidan tastes like
good scotch, and I can't help but reach my arms around his
neck as he kisses me hard and deep. Kissing cousins indeed. The
restaurant grows silent. If I open my eyes, I will see everyone
gawking at us. I will see Leticia Woolworth blush a deep purple
that perfectly matches her vintage Chanel suit. I will see Belinda
radiating with the injustice of it all and Felicity appear as if her
life has flashed before her eyes. But I'm too busy kissing to do
much noticing.

Finally Aidan pulls away, licking his lips like the fox who has just charmed the chickens right out of their feathers. I'm awash in lust and embarrassment, horrified that the clichéd hot guy can have this effect on my knees. I'm a grown-up, for God's sake, with a realistic view of the world. I'm too old for buckling knees. I straighten my dress and grab the microphone from Ms. Woolworth, whose eyes remain averted.

"I want to thank you all for coming," I say, "and for supporting our beloved Holt Hall. It was an honor to serve on the organizing committee this year, and I encourage all of you to get involved next year."

There are a few more things I'm supposed to say about future fund-raising efforts, but I find I don't care. Toward the back of the room I see Jason. He catches my eye, drapes an arm luxuriously over Belinda's bare shoulders, and gives me a smile of the not-so-nice variety.

Chapter 18

The laptop sits before me on the kitchen table. Beside it is a glass of Chardonnay with a few ice cubes. The night has brought no relief from the heat, and I think about dropping the ice cubes down my dress. I sip my drink. I stare at the ceiling. I pull on the hem of my Spanx suit.

On the way home, I gave Aidan a lecture on the inappropriateness of his kissing me like that in front of all those people. He laughed it off, told me I had nice lips and that I should not be so uptight. I asked him how a woman who writes about sex all day can possibly be uptight. He told me he didn't know but I was giving it a good effort.

After chewing on that for a few minutes, I changed the subject to dark places in New York City where we might look for Lily, because I no longer wanted to think about kissing.

Aidan threw out Lily's home address, her favorite coffee shop, a bistro where she has lunch. When I reminded him none of those places were dark, he gave me the silent treatment, which in turn, gave me time to focus on the pain lodged in my middle, as if someone had given me a swift kick with a steel-toed boot. Seeing Belinda and Jason together was not supposed to ruffle my feathers, and yet here I was with the bitter taste of jealousy in my mouth.

I move the cursor on the laptop and the machine whirs to life, but there are no new words. There is no chapter telling me exactly where to find Lily. The written story seems to have ended when Clarissa followed Aidan, who followed Lily. And my influence seems to have ended too. The characters I knew are hardly as they once were. They are like the difference between an eight-year-old huddled in your lap and a thirteen-year-old who will not let you enter her room for any reason.

All characters arise differently. Usually, before I start a new novel, I give myself a day off from suburbia and head into the city. I take an early train in and walk slowly downtown, following a slightly different route each time. I'm there to absorb the people.

I saw Lily in Grand Central Terminal. Of course, it wasn't the Lily we search for now but the woman upon whom that Lily would be based. She walked onto the main concourse just as I popped a plastic lid on my hot coffee and stuffed a heavily cream-cheesed bagel in my jacket pocket. As I turned toward the Forty-Second Street exit, there she was, curly strawberry

hair creating a halo around her Botticelli-perfect face. With a phone pressed to her ear and a leather briefcase in one hand, she gazed up at the heavens depicted on the terminal's famous ceiling.

"Oh," I said, drink frozen halfway to my face. "Perfect."

I was prepared to take my bagel and hoof it down to Union Square, maybe sit in the park for a while or shop one of the new stores that seem to appear almost daily. But as soon as I saw the redheaded woman, all of that changed. I had to follow her.

This wasn't the first time I'd stalked people who then, unbeknownst to them, had ended up in one of my novels, almost always eventually naked and in some rather compromising positions. If only they knew! Would they be horrified? Would it feel like infidelity even if they had no hand in it?

I thought about these things as I followed my mark out of the station and onto a Forty-Second Street teeming with people. Rush hour on foot was much more immediate than rush hour in a car. Using my elbows to push through the crowds, I worked hard to stay with her. How she kept up such a pace in those three-inch heels was beyond me, but she did. The lights seemed to magically change for her, so she never had to ease off. She just kept charging forward.

After a few blocks, she stopped at a coffee cart and took another phone call. I got in line immediately behind her.

"Hello," she said in a soft, lilting voice. "This is Lily. Oh, right. Hi, Brad."

She paused to listen to Brad. I inched closer.

"Sure," she said. "Five thirty still works great for me. Okay. I'll see you then."

There was a touch of the South in her voice, and my heart started to race. An innocent southern girl named Lily, running hard from her past, trying to make a go of it in big, bad New York City. I took another step forward, bumping her ever so slightly with the toe of my shoe. She turned toward me.

"So sorry," I said.

She smiled, flashing a set of perfect teeth and ripe lips that seemed kissed by summer raspberries. It was a genuine smile, not one offered as a distraction while the giver sizes you up and tries to figure out your angle. Because in New York, even if you just accidentally step on someone's toe, you *must* have an angle.

"It's okay," she said. I concentrated on her voice. Sometimes the sound of a character is the best way into her soul. It's hard to believe, I know, as characters in novels don't actually speak unless they've been subjected to the Hollywood blender, but for me a voice is crucial. I have to hear it in my head for the character to come alive on the page.

Before she returned to the phone call, I noted her cornflower-blue eyes and a subtle spray of freckles across her nose. The rest of her skin was creamy alabaster, as if she really did slop on the sunscreen and wear a big hat when her mother told her to. Lily was nearly flawless.

As she ordered a black coffee, I examined her clothes. A trendy suit jacket with bold geometric patterns and a tight, thigh-skimming skirt. Her stilettos were bright orange, and she wore a selection of chunky orange costume jewelry to match. Definitely not Wall Street, and no way she was a lawyer.

"Something creative," I said out loud. "Something that moves fast."

Marketing, of course. She's starting with a handful of little clients, maybe a group that sells organic perfume or shoes designed to tone your ass while you walk. But she has her eye on the bigger fish, the multinationals, the brands known even in the sandy deserts of Mali, and she's working hard to get them. Coffee in hand, she turned onto the Avenue of the Americas, and I watched her go.

She'll be fine, I thought at the time, whoever she is. A decent brain, a short skirt, and that hair will take her places.

I take another swallow of wine. I call Roger. After three rings, he answers.

"Something better be terribly wrong," Roger says. "It's two o'clock in the morning."

Have I really been sitting here that long? The wine bottle is almost empty. I guess so.

"Nothing's wrong," I say. "I have a question."

"I'm tired," he says. I ignore him.

"Tell me a dark place in New York City."

"My bedroom two minutes ago before you woke me up."

"I'm serious, Roger."

"Why are you on the phone with me and not in bed with your hot young thing? I saw him kiss you."

You and everyone else. Oh, I will have some explaining to do on Monday morning. I take another drink.

"He went to bed hours ago," I say.

"So?"

"And because he's perfect. And I have wrinkles and a kid and these awful brown age spots on my hands." Not to mention the spare tire.

"You're a real person, Sadie. Nothing wrong with that."

He has no idea just how right he is. About the "real person" part anyway.

"He's too young," I say. "He's probably never seen a woman with body hair. Anyway, what about dark places?"

"New York is never dark," Roger says, yawning. "You know, the city that never sleeps? Can I go back to bed now?"

"No! Just give me one place. Stretch if you have to. I'm desperate."

"If I live a thousand years, I will never understand the way your mind works," he says. "Okay. How about Central Park? The Ramble. I had a very dark and scary experience there once. The woman was a man who was a woman. Dear God. Dreadful. Good night, Sadie."

Roger hangs up. I lean back in my chair and consider the Ramble. It *is* dark and probably disconcerting if you're dropped there directly from an alternate reality. It's the kind of place Clarissa would come up with.

I repeat the word *ramble* over and over as I drag my tired

body up the stairs. Once in my room, I slowly undress, taking a moment to savor the joy I feel being released from the Spanx prison. I crawl into bed. But before I turn off the light, I take a small notebook from my night table and write the word *ramble* in big block letters.

Chapter 19

I wake to find I have a hangover and Aidan sitting on the side of my bed, one leg crossed loosely over the other. He wears a blue T-shirt, suit pants rolled casually at the ankle. His perfect feet are tucked into a pair of flipflops I have a vague memory of once seeing on Roger. Aidan has been rummaging through my closets.

"What time is it?" I groan.

"Seven thirty."

Ouch. I never look good at 7:30 in the morning, especially after two gin drinks, a bottle of wine, and five hours of sleep. Aidan holds my notebook. His shoulders are tense, his eyes red and tired.

"Do you think she's here?" he asks, shaking the page at me.

"Yes," I say quietly. A dark place. Sort of.

"*Why* is this happening?" he asks, fury in his voice. "What did I do to deserve this?"

It's a very good question and one I have asked a number of times since yesterday. To my mind, there are several possible answers. The first, and most compelling, is I'm having a midlife crisis and this is all part of a fantasy I've concocted. I've watched *American Beauty*. I see the signs. One moment everything is just as it always was and the next, utterly unfamiliar. You know, kind of like that Talking Heads song from the 1980s. But if I'm just sitting in the parking lot of Target imagining things, I've certainly gone overboard, even for me.

So that doesn't answer the question in a way that's satisfying. How about I was knocked unconscious and am in the ICU right now being treated for head trauma? Perhaps Roger and Allison and Greta stand at my bedside right now, wringing their hands in dismay over my condition. But I remember everything from the last day clear as a bell, and at no time did I fall down and hit my head. There is no interruption in the narrative.

The third possible answer is the most unsettling. Maybe all of this is really happening. Maybe the character of Aidan Hathaway has actually shown up here. Maybe everything is exactly as it appears.

But Aidan asked why it was happening to *him* and not why it was happening to me, and he's waiting very patiently for an answer. As if I have one to give.

"I don't know," I say finally. I'm hot and the room seems too small. We have to get out of here. We have to find Lily.

Aidan looks as though he might argue my answer, demand something more complete and satisfying, but he doesn't. Instead, he tears the page from the notebook. He crushes it into a tiny ball. He's a coiled spring ready to explode.

"So you think the Ramble is where we start looking?"

"Yes," I say.

Aidan pulls back my covers.

"Well, then get dressed," he barks. "Let's get going."

"Okay," I mutter. "I'm doing it. Go away."

"Brush your teeth, brush your hair. Do whatever. But get it done."

"Do you treat your stockholders this way?" I ask.

"No," he says. "I'm nice to them. They give me money, although according to you, I'm broke. I'll see you in the kitchen in five."

He must think I'm some sort of miracle worker. Five minutes allows for three minutes of additional yawning and maybe a tooth brushing. The hair will have to wait until some future date.

Downstairs, Greta, Aidan, and Allison sit around the kitchen table eating pancakes that smell heavenly. I kiss my daughter on the head and pile my plate with a respectable stack. I slip a pat of butter between each pair of pancakes and drench the whole mess with about a cup of warm syrup. There is no better cure for a hangover than a teetering pile of high-caloric food. If it comes with a side of fries, all the better.

Greta clears her throat. "Aidan tells me you'll be doing some . . . sightseeing in the city today?"

"Um, yes," I say. "And then I'll drop Allison off at Roger's for the night. Daddy says you're shopping?"

Allison does a little wiggle of happiness in her chair. "I can't wait!"

"How . . . interesting," Greta says.

"Yes," I say, stuffing my mouth with the glorious, fluffy pancakes. "It'll be fun."

"And hot," Greta adds.

Already the air outside the kitchen windows looks heavy and thick, and the remaining daffodils wilt where they stand.

"When's it going to end?" I ask. Greta always knows the weather details. She can talk barometric pressure and inversions and all that stuff.

"No one will say," she says. "So I suppose it ends when it ends."

Her pursed lips can only mean she disapproves of my plan to dump my daughter and my credit card with Roger and spend the rest of the afternoon frolicking around the city with my new young lover.

For a very split second, I consider coming clean to Greta. But an explanation would require time and finesse, and this morning I have neither. Plus it's possible that Greta would call 911 and I'd be parked in my own room at the fancy insane asylum by lunch.

As I inhale the pancakes, it occurs to me that I'm heading out into a world that no longer has anything in common with the world I woke up in yesterday. And while part of me pines

for yesterday, when everything made sense, another part of me is very aware of the shifting sands upon which I walk. It hurts my out-of-shape calves and the tiny muscles of my feet. But, and this is a big one, I feel all of my synapses firing. I see everything in sharp relief. Usually this only happens when I'm having a panic attack.

I can't say it out loud because it sounds crazy, but I'm excited about finding Lily. I'm excited that I will hear if her voice sounds like I intended it to. I want to see her face. Are her eyes really cornflower blue?

Since Roger left, I've had moments of great happiness with my daughter and moments of creative elation with my novels. I've seen wonderful movies and read books that kept me up all night. But joy, joy at the heart of Sadie Fuller, has been in short supply. It is not something I noticed or acknowledged until right now. And that is only because I feel the tendrils of fun creeping in around the edges. They are utterly inappropriate considering our current situation, but here they come, nonetheless.

Chapter 20

The gods must be smiling down on us because I find a parking space on Seventy-Third Street and Central Park West. When I open the car door, heat, the kind usually associated with a jet engine, rushes in. I gasp. Aidan blinks his eyes repeatedly.

"It's damn hot," he says. "Is it always this hot here?"

"No," I say, willing myself to step from the cool comfort of the minivan out onto the melting sidewalk. "But what's normal anymore?"

"Mom, why are we here?" Allison asks, unplugging from her iPod and looking around. "You're supposed to drop me at Dad's. Remember?"

And I would, darling, except Daddy isn't awake yet. Our divorce decree stipulated that I would never attempt to deliver his daughter to him until ten o'clock. He needs time to put away his incense and sex toys, and I have agreed to respect that.

"It's such a beautiful day," I say with a wide grin, "I thought we'd take a little walk in the park before going to Daddy's."

"A walk?" Allison is horrified. "It's, like, two hundred degrees already."

"But the flowers are beautiful this time of year," I say, grabbing her hand and dragging her as if she were a toddler and not almost the same height as I am.

As we enter the park, the daunting nature of our task hits me. The Ramble is thirty-eight acres of woods, rock outcroppings, and confusing foot trails. Birds sing. Daffodils bloom. There's a stream. It's huge. And we are guided by nothing more than a whim. A Roger whim. I see my own distress reflected on Aidan's face.

"Even if she is here, how the hell would we ever find her?" he asks.

"Who?" Allison asks.

"We're looking for a friend of Aidan's," I say quickly.

"Can't you call her?"

"Not exactly," I say.

"Well, where are you meeting her?"

"I don't know," says Aidan.

"So you're supposed to find a person here in Central Park just, like, somewhere?"

Sometimes it takes a child to put it all in perspective. A sense of doom settles over me. This will never work. We are flailing.

We continue walking along a wooded path. I feel I should

be shouting Lily's name, like when I call Perkins in from the backyard. We pass a fellow intrepid hiker.

"Excuse me," Aidan says. The walker is a middle-aged woman, dressed in expensive workout wear. Her face glistens with sweat. Her eyes drink in Aidan.

"Hi," she says, pretending Allison and I don't exist.

"I'm wondering if you've seen a woman," Aidan says with a perfect, knee-weakening smile. "Tall, red hair, perhaps wearing an orange dress and heels."

The woman is so taken with Aidan she almost quivers.

"Yes!" she says. "I did." She takes the opportunity to rest a confirming hand on his arm. She squeezes. She sighs. "On the path. Maybe a quarter mile? Sitting on a bench, I think." She grins as if she has just done something truly exceptional. Aidan rewards her with a wink.

"I'm grateful for your help," he says. We leave the woman to collect herself and possibly finish her aerobic morning walk. Although more likely, she's going to say "fuck it" and head for the nearest coffee shop to savor her brief encounter with the unforgettable Mr. Hathaway.

We continue down the wooded path. We pass runners and more walkers, people in pairs and people with dogs.

"I'm hot," Allison says. "This is boring. Can we go now?"

"Not quite," I say. "In a minute. And you know how much I love *bored*."

"I know, Mom," Allison says. "But I am. Even if I'm not allowed to say it."

We come to an intersection of pathways. A bench, "in memory of John Stark, who loved these woods," sits off to one side. It's empty. Aidan clenches his fists. Did he really think we'd just march into Central Park and find Lily? It can't be that easy or Ellen would have my head.

I approach a jogger who has stopped for a pull from his water bottle. I smile fetchingly. He stares at me blankly.

"Nice day for a run?" I ask.

"No," he says. Oh well. So much for small talk.

"Okay then," I say. "Maybe you can help me? We're looking for a woman in an orange dress. Tall. Red hair. Any chance you've seen her?"

The jogger chugs his water. Little rivers run down from the corners of his mouth and soak into his shirt.

"Yeah," he says after a pause. "I think I did. Real beauty. She was pretty close to the field over there. You know the one? She was messing with her shoes. I think one of her heels was broken."

I bet if I asked this man about what expression she wore on her face he could give me all the details. Men notice beautiful women. It's programmed into their DNA.

"Thanks!" I say brightly.

Quickly, I herd my reluctant crew forward. Our path is surrounded by dense vegetation and meandering streams. We pass under an old stone bridge that could have been conjured by Ralph Waldo Emerson. It's easy to forget the Ramble exists by design and is not the work of Mother Nature. We reach a bend in our path and turn onto another track.

"Mom," Allison whines. "We've been walking forever."

"No, honey," I say. "We're been walking for twenty minutes."

"Whatever," she says. I wonder, if I can find sex on Craigslist, can I sell a surly preteen? I'm sure.

"Just a little farther," I say to her as much as to myself. We reach another intersection.

"This is fruitless," Aidan hisses. He sweats only slightly, while I appear as if I just stepped out of a shower fully clothed. It's not fair.

"No," I say. "She's here. I just know it."

Once in a while, Roger and I would walk here. I'd admire the flowers, and he'd scope out places he could return to later for anonymous sexual encounters. It was all very domestic.

"How?" Aidan demands.

The same way I know when a scene is going to work. There's a small rush of adrenaline, an excitement, and suddenly my fingers cannot keep pace with my racing brain.

"Just trust me," I say. "This way." I choose the path on the right not because it is less traveled but because it is slightly more shaded. But still, it makes all the difference. As we walk, our path widens. A few hundred yards ahead a small field comes into view, littered with half-dressed sun worshipers.

"Hey, Mom," Allison says. She stops walking.

"Honey," I say before she can launch into a full-fledged hissy fit about our lovely walk in the saunalike conditions. "I'm sorry, but this is necessary. We have to find Aidan's friend. I know you aren't enjoying yourself just now, but sometimes in life you have to do things that are unpleasant."

"Jeez," she says. "I was just going to ask what kind of red hair and you get all crazy."

"What?"

"What kind of red hair does this person we're looking for have?" She enunciates each word as if I am an idiot. Eleven-year-old girls can be cruel. But I still outweigh her by a fairly large amount.

"Curly. Long," Aidan interrupts.

"Like that?" Allison points toward a bench off to the side of the walking path. Sitting on it is the woman from Grand Central, a cascade of strawberry-blond curls spilling down her slender back. She has the kind of hair that embraces humidity, as opposed to mine, which turns directly into a halo of frizz. Her skin is dewy like the morning grass, but the apples of her cheeks blaze red hot. From this distance, I can't see her eyes, but I know they will be cornflower blue. I imagine her orange dress bears telltale signs of a long night and a sweaty morning. She sees us and stands abruptly, hands on her hips, chin jutted out. I'd say this is the type of woman who looks great naked. She also looks totally pissed off.

"Where the *hell* have you been?" she snarls at us. We have found our dear Lily.

Chapter 21

Aidan rushes to Lily and sweeps her into his arms. It would be a very romantic scene, if not for Lily's reaction. She pushes him away. It's unambiguous. Aidan catches himself just before he tumbles to the ground.

"You owe me an explanation," she hisses at him. "How did I end up in the Ramble? I mean, I agree to meet for one lousy little drink and—*bam*—here I am in the goddamn woods! I woke up in the grass. In the dark. I was *complimented* on my cross-dressing skills. I was asked to *do* things."

She pokes Aidan in the chest, emphasizing each word, but I'm pretty sure it's not necessary. He gets it. He's crestfallen at her reaction.

"Why don't we give these two a minute?" I suggest to my shocked daughter. Adults don't behave like this in public. "Let's go and look at the tulips. I think I saw a ruffled Black Parrot over there. Those are really rare." Besides, there is a strange ringing in my ears, as if proximity to Lily is creating some sort of interference with my brain waves.

As we walk toward a bed of bedraggled tulips, Allison looks puzzled. "Are they boyfriend and girlfriend?" she asks.

"Aidan and Lily?" How do you properly explain lust to an eleven-year-old? The answer is you cannot. It is meaningless until you have the proper hormones coursing through your veins to experience it firsthand, and then it is all consuming. I expect this to happen to Allison any minute now. I live in fear.

"They like each other," I say.

"Do they play golf?" she asks.

"Golf?"

"Like Jane's mother and that man."

Oh, for fuck's sake. I hate Jane's mother. Can't she just be subtle about her desperation like the rest of us?

"No," I say. "I don't think they golf."

This makes Allison happy. Maybe she has a chance with the young stud mommy brought home from the hospital after all. She smiles.

Lily and Aidan appear in my peripheral vision. I expect them to be wrapped in each other's arms, gazing deeply and meaningfully into each other's eyes, but I see daylight between them. Aidan walks with his hands stuffed in his pockets, head bent, and Lily looks so tense I wonder if it's safe for us to be around her. She marches up to me while Aidan lags behind.

"So," she says, giving me the full frontal scowl. "I hear you're responsible for this mess I'm in. I only hope you know how to fix it."

Everyone stares at me, including my daughter. This is the part where I tell them what happens next.

"What?" I say, not because I didn't hear her demand an explanation but rather because I'd like a few more moments before she rips my head off. Lily is supposed to be sweet and innocent. I'd envisioned her starting her day with sun salutations and a few strategic namastes. But her transition from there to here has left her ferocious.

"This situation," she says, taking a step forward, "is unacceptable."

I take a step back.

"Aidan?" I say.

"I tried to explain to her what's going on," he says. "But she's really mad."

Allison is all ears. Whatever is happening, it is way more exciting than a nature walk. I pull out my phone and hand it to her.

"Call Daddy," I instruct. "Tell him we'll be there in forty-five minutes."

I turn back to Lily.

"Listen," I say quietly. "I don't know how to get you guys back because I didn't bring you here in the first place. So it's going to take some . . . exploration."

"Might I suggest you hurry up then?" she says.

I would love to hurry. I would hurry like mad if I only knew where I was hurrying to.

"Hey," Aidan says, tentatively resting an arm on Lily's shoulder. "It's going to be okay."

They make a stunning couple, the kind you expect to see on a Hollywood red carpet. But she's having none of it. She makes a face as if he smells bad and shoves his hand away. Two quick steps to the right and she's put enough space between them to make her point. Aidan sags. He bet his life, literally, on her feeling about him the way he does about her, and from the looks of it, it's a bet he might not win.

"No," Lily says. "I don't think it will be okay."

Just as I'm about to try and talk her out of her bad attitude, I get the sense we are being watched. The little hairs on the back of my neck stand up despite the oppressive heat, and suddenly the handful of joggers and walkers passing by all appear suspicious. They can't possibly be wearing sunglasses and baseball caps to cut the hideous late morning glare, can they? It must be something more insidious. Like they want to kill us.

On another path, off to our east, is a woman in a hat that is much too big and sunglasses that conceal ninety percent of her face. She wears skinny jeans and a flowing floral blouse. Her four-inch platform cork sandals are not something I would put on to go for a walk in the urban woods.

Is this Clarissa? Is she here to watch the fireworks as she said she intended to? Being this is the first time I've encountered an actual wicked witch, I have no idea what to expect. Will she pull

out a magic wand and turn me into a newt? Will she offer me a poisoned apple or a deal where I get to keep my life but she takes my voice . . . or my shoes or something? Perhaps I'll get lucky and the sultry air will clog up her magical powers, rendering her impotent.

Only one way to find out.

"I dropped something back there," I say to my people. "Give me a second."

I creep around on my very flat shoes and approach from behind. The woman is tall, especially with the heels, and thin, but she doesn't come by the thin naturally. It's gym thin. Cougar thin. Gorgeous twenty-something trainer thin.

I'm right behind her now. With one swift move, I knock the floppy hat off her head and jump back.

"Oh," she shrieks. She turns toward me. I'm prepared for anything. Except for this.

"*Belinda?*" I gasp. "What the hell are you doing here?"

Chapter 22

A t least Belinda has the good sense to look mortified.

"Well?" I demand. As she bends to retrieve the hat, her sunglasses slide off her nose. They are so huge you could deconstruct them and build a nice sunroom. It occurs to me she is in disguise.

"Well, it's a little complicated," she stammers, "and hard to explain." I hope so. It better be. "I don't know where to start." She kneads the hat with anxious hands, rolling its brim and squeezing. It will never be the same.

"The beginning," I suggest. I'm an odd combination of confused and relieved. While Belinda is great at starting rumors and can very easily ruin me that way, at least she is not going to cast a spell where I end up with a pig's tail and donkey ears. But that's the best part of this situation. "Go ahead. Start talking."

Belinda gestures toward Aidan, who is peering in our direction. I wave to him. He waves back, confused.

"Him," she says.

"What about him?"

"Last night," she says.

"What about last night?"

"At the fund-raiser," she says. "You walk in with this . . . god. Just like that. Out of nowhere. You. And then he kissed you. He kissed you and it looked like a movie scene. Except for your dress. That would never show up in a movie. But the kiss. That might."

I'm amazed at how comfortable some people are insulting others right to their faces.

"I still don't know how that has anything to do with anything," I say. Belinda looks like she's about to cry.

"I work out," she says with great distress. "I don't eat carbs or white sugar or . . . anything really. I deprive myself. It's *painful*. And then that beautiful man with the incredible body and thick head of hair, he kisses *you*! How can that be? It's *not* fair."

Belinda is the loneliest person I have ever met.

"I haven't been kissed like that in so long I can't even remember the last time," she adds with a sniffle.

"You should probably at least eat some whole grains," I say. "Maybe that would help you be more rational?"

She scowls. "I try, Sadie," she says. "I date. I go out with men. I want to like them. I want them to like me, but there's no magic. I never get that kiss. How did you do it?"

I invented the guy. I somehow had him transferred to my reality. I found him in Target. I sprang him from the hospital. I took him to the fund-raiser. We had cocktails. He kissed me. Easy.

Unprepared for this conversation, I offer her the same advice I give Allison from time to time.

"Be yourself, Belinda," I say. "Nobody is going to like you if you're pretending to be someone else."

I can hear you snorting with laughter. Who am I to tell another person to practice being genuine and love will follow? I, with the secret identity and the career none shall mention in polite company. I'm the worst kind of fraud. But you know how it goes, do as I say, not as I do.

Standing right in front of me in tippy heels, Belinda melts, and not from the heat. She's heartbroken over my kiss. Plus she's probably still hours away from her daily meal of a lettuce sandwich, hold the bread. Guilt, unbidden, arrives at my doorstep. Be nice, Sadie. You can do it.

"Guess what, Belinda?" I say. "You see that knockout redhead over there in the orange dress?" They watch us. I wave. Allison whispers something to Aidan. "*She's* the girlfriend." Or was. Things are a bit dicey right now. It could go either way.

"She's so . . . young," Belinda says, but with a look of relief. I'm not making it with the stud-muffin while she sits on the sidelines. Or runs in place on the treadmill.

"Yes, she is," I say.

"I haven't had sex in two years," she says, looking bewildered, as if she can't believe she's actually speaking about herself. A blast of superheated air blows by, and she picks her hat up off the ground and clamps it onto her head. "Not since the divorce. Not once. I think I want to, but I can't seem to find a partner." She starts to cry. Hot tears roll down her cheeks. "It wasn't supposed to be this way."

My heart does a leap of joy. I'm not happy because of Belinda's forced celibacy, possibly the one topic on which we can relate, but because if she hasn't had sex in two years, she did not end up fucking Jason in the front seat of his new red sports car in the parking lot of the Lake House Restaurant last night. I know it shouldn't matter, our relationship has boundaries, but still, I feel better.

"But you date," I say, because I need to say something and I want her to stop crying. "What about that guy from last night?"

"Jason Blair?"

Yes.

"He's nice," she says with a shrug. "But he doesn't, you know, totally do it for me. He needs to go to the gym more."

Belinda is the anti-me, and her not liking Jason and not sleeping with Jason is further evidence that Jason is an all-around good guy.

"So let me get this straight," I say. "You followed me to see if Aidan and I were together?"

She looks down at her feet.

"Belinda," I say.

"I know," she says. "I'm sorry. But you're not, right? Together? He's with the redhead."

Her eyes plead, but I refuse to prop her up further. Screw the guilt.

"Go home," I say. "Please."

Belinda's husband, Mark, left her for a woman young enough to be her own daughter. One night she showed up at my house long after Allison had gone to bed. She'd been crying, rivers of dried mascara caking her cheeks. I invited her in because I did not see I had any other choice. I sat her at my kitchen table. I made her decaffeinated green tea. I waited for her to tell me why she was there.

"I didn't know," she said finally. "Have you ever heard those stories about couples who are so attuned to each other that if one dies, the other knows it instantly, even before being told?"

I had not heard of such a thing, but I said yes anyway. This was going to be a monologue. My job was to sip tea and offer affirmations at the correct intervals. If she started crying again, I'd hand her a box of Kleenex.

"Well, Mark was fucking that model for almost six months and I had no idea," she continued. "He had an apartment in New York that I didn't know about! Couldn't the universe have given me a sign? I'm a good person. If it was more blow jobs he wanted, I could have done that."

She started to cry. I handed her the tissues.

"I'm sorry, Sadie," she whimpered. "I know you had a gay husband, so you probably can't understand any of what I'm saying."

I moved the tissue box just beyond her reach. I took her half-full mug of tea, got up, and placed it in the sink. I stretched. I yawned. I congratulated myself for not telling her to go fuck herself.

"I'm really tired, Belinda," I said. "Thanks for stopping by. I hope you feel better. I really do."

Belinda pushed back from the table slowly. It was a turning point for us. We were not going to be friends. The underwear model was not the great leveler she could have been. Belinda still found me inferior. So inferior, in fact, that she had to follow me to Central Park to make sure I wasn't sleeping with a younger, good-looking man because her ego, or what was left of it, simply could not absorb that blow. Had she arrived to find me groping Aidan in the shadows of the Ramble, she would have died on the spot.

To the west, the sky grows dark, as if a thunderstorm might soon release us from the heat. Allison stands between Aidan and Lily, acting as a human barrier, totally unaware. Lily's arms are crossed against her chest, a look as dark as the incoming storm on her face. Aidan seems confused, tired. None of this makes sense. Mopping my forehead with a stale tissue excavated from my giant purse, I return to the fold.

"Time to head to Daddy's, okay?" I say.

Allison nods, peering around me. "Was that Mrs. Connors you were talking to over there?" she asks.

"Yes," I say with too much enthusiasm. "Isn't that funny? She was here to see those rare tulips, too. What a coincidence, right? We probably should have carpooled. Great! Okay, troops, to the car!"

Each step is a trial. My hair is plastered to the back of my neck. In the field to our right, visitors lie very still, hoping to catch a breeze. My mind registers that there are a lot of people for this time of day and in this heat.

I feel her before I see her. She's a shocking cold streak, an unexpected chill. Standing in the middle of the field, she wears all black, her dark hair flowing around her like a wedding veil gone Goth. She is still some distance away, but our eyes find each other despite the crowd and I feel immediately nauseous. It's the very same sensation I experienced in my kitchen just yesterday morning, back when my life did not resemble a freak show. I grab Aidan by the arm, sinking my short nails deep into his skin. Just to make sure he's paying proper attention.

"Hey, that hurts," he says. "What are you doing?"

I point. Aidan looks, blinks, looks again.

"Oh shit," he says.

Yes. That sums it up rather eloquently.

Chapter 23

That's her!" Lily screams, sending the lounging New Yorkers up onto their elbows. Clarissa smiles at us across the distance. The smile gives me instant chills. If I had any control over this story, Aidan would now draw his sword and step forward to defend us in the face of evil.

But no. He positions himself so it's clear I'm the leader of this gang. Clarissa moves toward us, almost as if she is floating an inch above the grass. Lily looks terrified. Allison, still in possession of my phone, is oblivious. My mouth tastes of fear. It's cottony and dry, and I lick my lips. This is entirely new territory. I find myself wishing I had just one little superpower, like invisibility or the ability to make fire fly from my fingertips. Hell, I'd take simple flight at this point.

Clarissa comes closer. I stand perfectly still, as if I've grown roots. Behind me, Aidan mumbles platitudes. Or maybe he's pleading. I can't tell. Lily appears to be the only one thinking straight.

"You bitch!" she yells at Clarissa. "How dare you do this? How dare you mess with my life?"

Aidan snaps out of it long enough to restrain Lily with both arms as she struggles to break free. She wants to throw herself at Clarissa and claw her eyes out. Aidan begins to sweat with the effort of holding her.

Clarissa laughs. It's a terrible sound, high and sharp, and it rattles something deep in my chest. I want to cover my ears. The sound grows louder. The crowd, scattered around the lawn, begins to take on form. Do they know? Are they going to rise up against the malevolent witch in their presence? It's such a strange thought, but it *is* New York. Anything can happen.

"You should be quiet," Clarissa says. Her voice throws me back on my heels. It's so familiar, and yet I know I've never heard it before. Lily goes immediately limp and silent, as if all the air has been sucked from her lungs. Aidan holds her up, a rag doll in his arms.

Clarissa does not go for Aidan and Lily. She comes right to me. My heart pounds so desperately I swear I can see it through my shirt. I clasp my hands together in front of me as if ready to fend off physical blows.

Clarissa stops. She's taller than I am by about five inches, but she wears heels, so maybe flat-footed we're the same. There are faint crow's-feet at her eyes and laugh lines around her mouth, although I get the distinct feeling they are not the result of excessive hilarity. Her thick mascara and red lipstick would be more appropriate for a night out than for a morning jaunt around the park. And I can't believe she has not passed out from heatstroke in the black, long-sleeved, form-fitting dress.

Clarissa was probably beautiful at some point. She was probably softer and less angular and less pissed off. But now she reminds me of the sharp, middle-aged suburban women I see pushing carts up and down the aisles of Whole Foods.

"You," she says, standing inches from me, peering into my face. "You think you can make everything better?"

My lips move, but no sound comes out.

"They're already doomed," she says. "Once you fall in love, you have everything to lose."

"No," I whisper.

"You must understand it's not enough to simply reunite the lovebirds. You need the magic, a spell," she says, circling me. "Words. Important words. But the chances of you, of all people, figuring them out, well, it wouldn't be fun if it were easy, now, would it?"

Clarissa drags a long red fingernail across my shoulder blades. Something in her touch drops my body temperature precipitously, and I shiver. I've fallen into a nightmare. There is light, if only I could reach it. But I remain planted in the concrete. In my peripheral vision, I see Aidan and Lily. Lily is still limp, but her eyes are open. Aidan stares at Clarissa and me as though he's in a trance. If I had a brick in my purse, I would heave it at him.

"We still have twenty-four hours," I stammer.

Darkness clouds Clarissa's face. Her red lips squeeze into a tight line. Perhaps I've said the wrong thing.

"Twenty-two hours and thirty-seven minutes," she snaps. "To be exact."

I shrink back. Any gusto I had is gone. I'm no better than the Cowardly Lion, quaking in my tennis shoes.

"Why are you here?" Aidan shouts suddenly. "What do you want from me? I don't even *know* you!"

The sound of his voice cracks the nasty veneer of Clarissa's face ever so slightly. Her eyes show evidence of heartbreak, the kind with which I am familiar.

"You're just saying that to hurt me," she says dismissively. "But once you remember, you'll see things my way. As for right now, I'm simply checking in to make sure you don't *need* anything." She waves a hand before her face, and Lily clutches her stomach as if in acute pain. Just as quickly, Clarissa lowers her hand, and Lily returns to normal.

This is bad. Really, very bad. But there are rules.

"We have twenty-two hours and thirty-seven minutes left to figure out your spell," I say. "That's how you said it would go." If Clarissa were able to fudge the time, the plot of this story would go straight to hell. Where's the tension, the conflict, if Clarissa can change the terms of the bet on the fly? The rules exist for a reason, and to them we must adhere.

Clarissa narrows her eyes, which is evidence enough that I'm right.

"He's mine," she whispers. "And after you fail, he will be mine forever."

I have no good comeback. If I had an hour, the peace and quiet of my office, and a strong espresso, I might be able to come up with something. But right now, the best I can do is borrow from my eleven-year-old.

"Whatever," I say.

Clarissa turns toward Aidan and Lily. I have no idea what she's going to do. Hurl fireballs? Whip up a tornado? Aidan wraps his arms protectively around Lily. She makes no attempt to wrestle herself free. Maybe this will melt the ice between them. They really do look so good together, even in the face of evil and all that.

"Don't come any closer," Aidan warns.

Again, the laugh, like nails on a chalkboard.

"My darling," Clarissa says. "Don't look at me like that. You know this is for the best."

"You're crazy," Aidan growls. "I don't know who you are or what you're up to, but it won't work."

Clarissa doesn't like this idea at all. Her hand starts to come up, the one I will from this day forward associate with a very bad stomachache. Lily moans.

"Hey, Mom!" Allison's voice reaches me as if from another dimension. "Check it out!"

Allison, playing Angry Birds, has wandered onto the field. A surge of music, coming suddenly and loudly from over my left shoulder, takes me by surprise. For a moment, I think it is Clarissa's sinister theme music, somehow broadcast directly into my brain. But a man with dreadlocks and a filthy Bob Marley T-shirt appears, holding a boom box over his head. The people who were lounging on the grass rise and begin to form neat rows. A TV crew appears on the far side of the field. Have the media been notified about the recent break in reality? As everyone spreads out to encompass much of the field, we are pushed to one side. Clarissa is shoved in the opposite direction. The music builds. The lined-up people strike a variety of poses. Flash mob.

And this is why I love New York City, even if I did once find a dead guy in my vestibule.

Clarissa eyes the newsman with the video camera making his way into the crowd, filming this "spontaneous" event. And suddenly I have a thought. In fictional worlds, witches live quietly among us. They do not want to be known. They do not want to be on television. My priority now is to figure out Clarissa's magic words or spell, and if she is hot on our heels, our chances of succeeding at our task drop precipitously. Ask anyone. Being chased around by a witch can be very distracting.

So I take the opportunity for what it is worth.

"I think it's time to go," I say.

"But I want to watch the dancers," Allison protests.

"We have to get you to Daddy's," I say. "We don't want him to worry."

"I'll text him," she says. "Who was that lady in the dress?"

"Nobody," I say.

"Wasn't she hot?" Allison asks.

"Text your father and tell him we're on our way," I say, taking her by the elbow and maneuvering her away from the crowd. Lily and Aidan fall in behind us. "Hey, and then maybe you can download that music app you were telling me about last week?"

"You said I couldn't have it," Allison says.

"Well, I just changed my mind," I say. "How about that?"

Technology has many uses. One of them is redirecting a child's attention. Works like magic. And let's hope it's not the only magic I can conjure in the next twenty-two hours and thirty-seven minutes.

Chapter 24

The four of us arrive at Roger's apartment, where I land a spot right in front of the building's door. In normal circumstances, such a seismic shift in my parking karma would leave me giddy. But today I simply see it as further evidence the world is not as it should be. I proceed to wrestle my phone out of Allison's hands. I gave her permission to download the music app, but she's eleven and has been in possession of my phone for the entire ride to Roger's apartment. Who knows what sorts of mysteries now reside on it?

In the backseat, Lily sits huddled against the door, eyes closed, trying to make herself as small as possible. She's hoping if she concentrates hard enough, she can reverse the last day's events and wake up in her own bed, in her own apartment, with her own stuff. A part of her knows this is not going to happen, but she stays rolled in a tight ball anyway, hovering somewhere between hope and despair.

As much as I'd like to leave Lily and Aidan here in the car as I escort Allison upstairs to Roger's, I won't. I think we gave Clarissa the slip at the park, but I can't be one hundred percent sure. I'm afraid of what she will do to the two of them if I am not in the way. A vision of a cat playing with a half-dead mouse comes to mind.

Beside me in the passenger seat, Aidan looks bereft.

"You don't remember her at all?" I ask quietly.

Aidan shakes his head.

"A disgruntled client? A fired employee?"

"No," he says. "I have no idea who she is."

"Well," I say. "She certainly knows you."

"Mistaken identity."

"I doubt it," I say. "She seems sure."

"If I give myself up, do you think you'd all be safe?" he asks.

"Hard to say. It would mess up her game, and she seems to be enjoying herself. Some people are like that."

I pull open the van door. A waft of air, tinged with the stink of baked garbage, greets us.

"This is turning into such a fun day," Aidan says with a grimace.

Allison climbs out of her seat and across Lily to exit street-side. As she does this, her overnight bag clocks Lily in the face. Lily's eyes well up, and I suspect it is not from pain.

"Come on," I say. "We'll get out of New York after we drop

Allison. It's easier to think in the country." My redheaded, heart-broken creation doesn't look at me. She wipes her eyes, and we file into Roger's building.

Roger lives in a very tight one-bedroom with a single window that looks out on the concrete wall of the building beside it. His entire bedroom would fit nicely in my closet. It's important to note that Roger did not want to live in an apartment where he had to store his yoga mats in the stall shower. No. He had much grander ideas, but our divorce mediator set his monthly living allowance at five thousand dollars and refused to be swayed by his pouting.

"This will motivate you to focus on making a success out of your yoga studio," she told him. "And you'll feel better about yourself."

I didn't mention to her that Roger would not know self-doubt if it bit him on the ass, but he was known to experience acute agony if denied access to a Marc Jacobs trunk show. However, Roger has his priorities. If you peer into his kitchen cabinets, you will not find any food. You will find neatly stacked Marc Jacobs shirts. When Allison visits, Roger sleeps on the couch.

Allison hugs him hard when he opens the door. He buries his face in her hair and breathes her in. He loves his little girl more than anything, and for that, I will always be grateful. When Roger looks up, his eyes come to rest on Lily, standing behind Allison with the rest of us. He smiles graciously, raising an eyebrow in my direction, and ushers us in.

"Will you excuse us for a moment?" he says once we are all inside. He drags me by the upper arm into the bathroom, the only place in the apartment with an actual door.

"Why is that man still hanging around?" Roger whispers. It's a door, yes, but it's thin as paper.

I shrug.

"And where did Princess Ariel come from?"

I shrug again. Roger squeezes my arm. He can do handstands on his fingertips, so it hurts.

"You told me at the fund-raiser, he'd be gone by morning."

"I did?"

"I thought so," Roger says.

"Maybe you just think I did," I say. "You're hurting my arm, you know."

"Sorry," Roger says, releasing me. "I'm concerned, that's all. You're behaving strangely, and normally you're so . . . normal. Are you feeling okay?"

No. I'm not okay. I have not been okay for years. I'm forty-six and alone, except I'm never alone. I'm in charge of everything and I don't want to be. I'm tired. My body feels old, and it sags in places I wish it wouldn't. I want more joy. I want integration. I want to figure out the proper spell to return my beautiful creations to their beautiful world so they can make beautiful love and I can maybe eke out a sequel, so I can swing Allison's Holt Hall tuition next year. How's that?

"I'm fine," I say. "Just trying to help out those less fortunate than me."

"Oh please," Roger says. We are close. I mean, he saw me have a baby, and that could not have been pretty. But I cannot share this with him. It goes too deep into my gray matter.

I push open the bathroom door before he can pin me down and, with a big grin on my face, enter the tiny living area. Allison is busy showing Aidan Roger's collection of antique snow globes. Yes, he had them when we got married. No, I did not see the implications for my sex life. Lily stares out the window at the concrete wall. The window air-conditioning unit whines in desperation.

I hug Allison.

"You can each buy one thing," I say, handing Roger my credit card. "And that one thing must cost less than a hundred dollars."

"Okay, Mom."

"Okay, Sadie."

I kiss everyone, round up my posse, and head out the door.

"I like Allison," Aidan says as we head back to the car. "She's got some spunk to her."

"She does," I agree. "Girls need it these days. Life has changed a lot since I was a kid."

Lily stops on the sidewalk. She places both hands on her hips and stares me down.

"What?" I say.

"Lily?" Aidan asks.

"It just occurred to me, Aidan," she says, "that we know next to nothing about our *host*. Isn't that curious?"

"I guess," Aidan says, but he doesn't sound sure because what does he need to know about me other than how I intend to get him the fuck out of this place?

"We should go," I say.

Lily plants her feet.

"No," she says. "I'm not going anywhere until you give us some details. Maybe this is all a giant brainwashing scam to cheat us out of . . ." She pauses, casting around for something to fill in the blank.

"Yeah," I say, "that about sums up what you've got."

"Come on, Lily," Aidan says, taking her arm. "It's hot out here."

And for the record, in fiction, no one cares about the authors, except in very rare circumstances. We do not live in fear of paparazzi jumping out of our shrubs when we attempt to leave the house. And that is how it should be. Because if the author can't stay out of the way of her story, she had better go off and write a memoir or something.

"Hey," I say. "You want to find out what happens if we can't figure out that spell? We have less than twenty-four hours and not a clue, and I'd say *that's* what you should be worrying about, wouldn't you?"

This seems to get through. Reluctantly, Lily gives in and follows us to the car. Fortunately, it's the kind of day on which even the most stubborn of positions can be broken by the need for air-conditioning.

Chapter 25

The minivan is quiet as we cross the invisible line from urban to suburban. Suddenly, there are more trees and no sidewalks and even the occasional smooth stretch of highway. I sit in the front alone. In the rearview I can see Aidan and Lily. He whispers in her ear, runs a hand down her thigh. She appears to be softening. I, however, can think only of spells and incantations and charms, anything that might be considered mystical or magical.

But it's not easy. The extent of my knowledge on the subject comes from Disney. Nowhere else can you find such a collection of modern-day, spell-chanting witches. They take many forms, but most are tall and lean and pinched and bitter. They sport eyebrows you could cut yourself on. They scheme and plot and throw themselves in love's path whenever possible. Oftentimes, it's about revenge for getting old or losing power, which are kind of the same thing when you think about it. Sometimes they simply hate the beautiful young princess's happiness, an emotion no longer able to root in their cold, dark hearts.

But none of that is important. What's important is what they *say*. I should have paid more attention. When I sat beside Allison on the couch, watching *The Little Mermaid* for the forty thousandth time, I should have listened to what Ursula sang when she stole Ariel's voice. But instead I was typing away on my keyboard, working, and smiling at Allison every time she told me I had to watch a specific part because it was awesome. I should have been much more present. I should have skipped the multitasking. I regret that now.

To hedge my bets, I put my heels together, carefully, so as not to drive the minivan into a ditch, and click them three times. There's no place like home. There's no place like home. There's no place like home.

I wait for a dreamy bubble of light to appear, carrying a good witch or a fairy godmother who will fix everything, but of course, this does not happen. My characters still occupy the backseat. However, we are not completely without miracles. Lily smiles. Or half-smiles. And while I can't see Aidan's hand, I have a sneaking suspicion I know in what direction it has traveled.

I squirm. I turn up the music. I return to obsessing over spells. If I'm the default team leader here, I'd better come up with something fast. My daughter has programmed every music outlet in my car to play the pop songs she favors. It creates a nice bar-

rier around me, and I drive, barely conscious of my actions. This route is automatic, just like the ride to school. On the radio a twenty-year-old pop singer complains about love and how she's alone again, and as she does, an audible gasp escapes me.

I need help.

Now these are three little words I rarely dare utter, because who would I ask? Who would listen? Roger is out. Greta is out. I don't have the types of girlfriends I call "sisters" and spill my guts to on a regular basis, so that leaves . . . Jason.

Jason? I run a nervous hand through my sweaty hair. Are you insane, Sadie? Jason is someone you have sex with. Yes, I know he likes me well enough. He would not continue to show up at my house every Friday morning, bearing sandwiches, if he didn't. But Jason and I are about the physical, not deep conversation. Not help.

For the first time, the limitations of our relationship sit like a rock in my stomach. I don't want to tell just anyone about my situation, I want to tell Jason. This, coupled with my reaction to seeing him last night with Belinda, is cause for concern.

In the backseat, Aidan kisses Lily. If *Stolen Secrets* had proceeded in a normal fashion, I would have had them in positions much more compromising than a single kiss. So why does it make me uncomfortable? I clear my throat. Aidan pulls away. Lily's eyes remain closed, her luscious lips parted ever so slightly.

"Spells!" I bark at them. "Do you know any? Maybe a charm or two?"

"Clarissa's in your book," Aidan says, still gazing at Lily. "Shouldn't you know the answer?"

"No," I shout.

I slam on the brakes and skid off the highway and onto the sandy shoulder. Aidan and Lily pitch forward.

"Jesus, Sadie!"

"I didn't create Clarissa!" I say. "She just showed up and made a mess of things!"

Suddenly the minivan is too small. I push open the door and fall out, the fingers of panic clawing at my throat. If I didn't create Clarissa, where did she come from? It doesn't make any sense, no matter which angle I approach it from.

I brace myself against the hood of the minivan, arms straight out, propping me up. The metal is so hot I'm at risk of burning my palms, but I don't care. There's a thought, down deep in the murky water of my mind, pushing toward the surface, but I can't quite hook it.

"Come on," I say. "What the hell is it? What can't I see?"

Aidan hops out of the car.

"Sadie?"

I ignore him. I pace alongside the minivan. Grit, kicked up from the traffic flying by on the highway, covers me. I will not be able to get away with wearing the skort for yet another day.

"I wish we were more helpful," he says.

I keep pacing. I remember my obstetrician telling me, when Allison was two weeks late, that if I moved around it might help the baby be born. Well, maybe the same logic applies here. If I

keep moving, perhaps the thought I'm grasping for will break free and be born. I pace faster. Aidan blocks my way.

"Sadie," he says. "Please. It's hot as hell. Get back in the car."

"What was it you said?" I ask him.

"Get back in the car?"

"No, before that!"

"That it's your book and you should know the answer?"

And there it is. Fully formed.

"Yes!" I grab him by the shoulders and shake him. "Of course I should know the answer! Paranormal!"

"I have no idea what you're talking about, but I demand you get back in the car this instant."

I laugh insanely. I spin around in the dirt. I hug Aidan.

"Paranormal," I say again.

"Get in the car."

I do as I'm told. Aidan joins me in the front seat, a look of deep concern on his face. It's the same one Roger wore in the bathroom not an hour earlier.

"Paranormal," I repeat. "I can't believe I didn't think of it earlier."

"Will you stop saying that word? Or at least explain what the hell you mean?"

Okay. Sure. Listen to this.

I have a friend, an older man, who writes mysteries and is quite well known. Every few months we get together for drinks and complain about the business of publishing. This friend has had twenty-four novels hit the *New York Times* bestseller list. He has rabid fans. He has multiple houses. He has a very young wife. He is the epitome of success for an author. But is he happy? Yes, mostly, but for the fact that the same newspaper upon whose bestseller list he so frequently appears refuses to review his work. It's a thorn in his side.

"Snobs," he yells. "Bastards."

He has tried different strategies to get them to pay attention, but they turn up their noses and instead focus on "real" literature. I have told him that until a genre writer—mystery, political thriller, western, whatever—wins the Nobel Prize in Literature, we will be out in the critical cold. I have told him to buy a warm parka and take comfort from his outstanding success. But it doesn't matter what I say. He's still angry.

I myself am perfectly happy to have robust sales and be critically ignored, but I understand his pain because writing a good mystery is hard. Writing a good romance is hard. Writing a believable sex scene is hard. Yes, the results vary, but the process is still a long and delicate one.

This was not something I appreciated on a visceral level until I tried to write a paranormal romance. I'd done quite well with straight romance and then with the erotica, so my agent, always looking out for my professional future, suggested paranormal.

"It's all the rage," Liz Stelow said. "It's huge. Enormous. And I don't mean that in a double entendre way. So look, when Alexi at Harper calls me and says she wants something for her spring

catalog next year, I immediately think of you. You bang out a few books a year easy. Want to have a go at this?"

I was two years post-Kurt and two months shy of meeting Roger, so I certainly had the time. But the problem was I didn't read paranormal. I wasn't even exactly sure what it was.

"Vampires?" I asked.

"Not necessarily," she said. "You could do witches or people with magical powers or some sort of sensitive zombie, I suppose."

Remember, we were two adults having this conversation.

"And it needs hot, young things in it," she added, "but you're really good at those."

I was. It was true. My feathers fluffed up with pride.

"Just, you know, don't skimp on the otherworldliness. Okay?"

My feathers collapsed. Clearly, Liz didn't read paranormal any more than I did. But I'd transitioned from one genre to another before, so I figured paranormal would be no big deal.

I jumped in with both feet. I read the bestsellers. I studied the craft, and then I sat down at my laptop to write a story about two witches, sisters and rivals, who are in a battle for the soul of a mortal man. A very good-looking mortal man, of course, and scantily clad when possible.

From the beginning I had delusions of grandeur. I saw sequels, a television series, a blockbuster summer movie, Barbie dolls and action figures. But then reality showed up rather inconveniently.

As it turns out, genre writing is not interchangeable. If it were, believe me, we'd all be writing legal thrillers or novels about Russian spies. But each genre requires a gift, a skill that might not be translatable to another world.

I could not write the book. I liked my witches. They were tart and sassy and mean as hell to each other. They paraded around their East Side castle like divas, in high heels and gowns, no matter what time of day. The man in question was a policeman, on a beat in their neighborhood. And oh, they loved him! It should have been easy. It should have followed the same rules as romance or erotica. But it did not. I couldn't get the tone right or the nuance or the comedy. My manuscript wasn't fun. It was dreary and dark. It did not read like the work of Sadie Fuller or K. T. Briggs. In short, it was awful.

"What do you mean you can't do it, Sadie?" Liz shrieked when I admitted my failure.

"It's too different," I said.

"It's not at all," she said. "You're just overthinking it."

No. I once heard a critically acclaimed novelist proclaim he worked on a single sentence for a full year because he could not get it quite right. That's overthinking it. I was just accepting defeat before I got to the painful part.

"I can't do it," I repeated.

"Fine," Liz said in a huff. "If you can't, I'll find someone who can."

Of all the terrible things to say, that was the worst. Briefly, I reconsidered my decision to abandon the paranormal uni-

verse, but by then it was too late. Liz had hung up. I sat at my desk for a few minutes, chewing on my fingernails. Was my career over?

Of course not. I had several good ideas on deck for erotic romances. I just had to choose one and get started. And that's exactly what I did.

The air in the minivan is damp and stale. Aidan and Lily stare at me, blank looks upon their wrinkle-free faces.

"And?" Aidan asks as I finish my tale. I have obviously not made myself clear.

"The witches," I say.

Lily pushes up between the front seats. She glows with sweat, but it looks nice, like it's mixed with glitter or pixie dust.

"What about the witches, Sadie?"

"Clarissa was one of the sisters. I wrote her *before*."

Chapter 26

feel we've had a breakthrough, but my passengers don't seem to appreciate that fact. They appear thoroughly confused.

"What exactly do you mean by that?" Aidan asks.

"I did create her, as you suggested, just not for *Stolen Secrets*. I still can't get a handle on why she's after you, Aidan, but there is one thing I do know."

"And what's that?" They're skeptical, understandably. I haven't been a huge help thus far.

"The manuscript, the paranormal one with Clarissa, had spells," I say. "Lots of spells." And they all rhymed. Not that it matters, but I've always been fond of the rhyming couplet. I came up with spells everywhere, in the shower, at the market, out to dinner. It was the only part of the paranormal experience I really enjoyed.

"And you think one of them will send us back?"

"Yes," I say. "She banished people in that story, so the right spell just has to be there." Plus I have no plan B, so I feel I ought to sell this one for all it's worth.

"Do you remember them?" Lily asks, anxious.

"Not off the top of my head," I say. But there are days I can't remember what I had for lunch, so this doesn't seem significant. "They're written down somewhere. I just need to find the manuscript or my notes."

My left eye twitches. Finding the manuscript or my notes is actually much scarier than it sounds. Fortunately, before anyone asks for additional information on that topic, my cell phone rings.

"Hello?" I say.

"Hi, Sadie. It's Jason."

"Hi, Jason," I say, swallowing. I'm nervous. Why am I nervous?

"Are you home?"

"In the car."

"You shouldn't talk on the phone in the car. It's a huge ticket, plus it's dangerous."

"Bluetooth," I lie.

"How are you?" he asks.

Not very well.

"Fine," I say.

"Hey," he says, "about last night. It was a blind date. The wife of a colleague set me up, and I couldn't say no. I'm sorry it turned out to be your neighbor and your, ah, fund-raiser."

"Did you have fun?" I ask. I've heard Belinda's side of the story. Now I want to hear his.

"Well," Jason says. "I don't think Belinda is really my type. She can't seem to talk about anything but what she did at the gym and who is cheating on whom. It was depressing."

Plus she's a stalker.

"I'm sorry you didn't have a good time," I say. But I'm not. Not even a little.

There's a pause. Jason clears his throat like he's about to launch into prepared remarks.

"So how about you? Did you enjoy the evening with your . . . young man? That was quite a kiss he laid on you."

There's a hint of pain and jealousy in his voice. Are we traveling on a two-way street?

"It was nothing," I say quickly. "The cocktails were pretty strong. Anyway, we just picked up his girlfriend in New York."

From Jason, an audible sigh of relief. This conversation is drawing lines around our relationship. It's forcing definition. In the silence that follows, we both consider what this means.

"Well," Jason says finally, "I'm glad to hear he has company. He's very . . ."

"Good looking?" I say.

"Yes," Jason laughs. "That might be the word for it. I was thinking I would come over."

"To my house? Now?"

"Yes. Well, when you get home. I want to talk to you about something."

I hate when people say that. It's never anything good. Perhaps what I interpreted as jealousy at the kiss is really disgust. Maybe he's done with me. I should tell him no, he cannot come over. I should remind him we only see each other on Friday mornings, but I hear myself say, "Sure. We should be home in fifteen minutes." The way today is going, there's a good chance Belinda will see his car and take up residence in the shrubs outside of the house. How dare I take up with a man she doesn't want for herself?

We bounce up the rutted driveway and park outside the garage. Greta stands in the front doorway. Although she wears the same sensible wool dress and shoes she wears every day, she does not appear overheated. Greta takes in the scene as Aidan helps Lily from the car.

"The girlfriend," I whisper to Greta. "Her name is Lily."

"And she's a little overdressed for a Saturday afternoon," Greta says at full volume.

Aidan, awash in chivalry, helps his ladylove navigate the uneven flagstone path to the front door. They both look exhausted, red eyed, and frayed around the edges. I've noticed that beautiful people can lack a certain robustness we mere mortals have in spades.

"Why don't you show Lily the guest room?" I say to Aidan. "You can get cleaned up."

"And you'll look for the manuscript with the spells?" His face is five years older than it was yesterday. The youthful arrogance he displayed while propositioning me in my kitchen has faded. Real life, such as it is, can be hard.

"Yes," I say. Greta is suddenly at my shoulder.

"Is something missing?" she asks. Nothing is ever missing in our house because Greta has a library catalog for a brain. If you ask her for the scissors she will provide turn by turn directions to the kitchen drawer where said scissors reside. She can probably reel off their serial numbers too, if pressed. It's a gift I do not possess. If Greta did not return my car keys to the table by the front door each night, I'd never leave the house.

I know if I asked her to find me a discarded unfinished manuscript that didn't even earn itself a working title, she could. But I don't want to be under her watchful eye. It will only remind me that I'm involved with something I cannot explain and which makes no sense at all.

"No," I say, "nothing's lost. Just some pages I want to show our guests."

Greta swings the door wide and ushers us in. Within moments, Aidan and Lily will have fluffy towels, a clean change of clothes, and a selection of travel-size toiletries from which to choose. Aidan slips a strong arm around Lily's waist. There is no daylight between them now.

I follow them upstairs and turn off at my office. Gently, I close the door. It smells dank and hot, as if beyond the reach of air-conditioning. I sit down at my desk. I run my hands over the wood. My office may be a sanctuary of sorts, but it is also a mess. There are piles of papers, magazines, books, coffee cups, scraps of Allison's homework, junk mail, and stale bagel parts covering almost every surface. I don't allow Greta in here because first, I'm afraid it would give her a heart attack, and second, I'd never find anything ever again. And I know where things are in here. Sort of.

By my calculations I created Clarissa and Evangeline twelve years ago. Nowadays, I'm fully electronic and proud of it. With the exception of my bedside notebook, used only for late night emergencies, I take notes exclusively on a tablet or my smartphone, and I write only on my laptop. But back in the dark ages, things were different. Back then I had a system, if you could call it that. The system was a little black notebook I tried to carry on my person everywhere I went. If something struck me, I'd write it down. It might be the way a person walked or a certain environment that was perfect for a new scene. Sometimes it was a snippet of dialogue picked up in the store or on the train. When I sat down to write, I would comb this notebook for bits to support whatever story idea I was pursuing. It was a treasure chest of details.

But sometimes I'd forget the notebook and I'd resort to jotting down notes on cash register receipts or coffee shop napkins or whatever piece of paper was close at hand. I'd stuff these notes in my purse and forget about them until the next time I needed something to write on. My office was adrift in little pieces of paper, none of which could be thrown out because they might just hold the key to a particular project.

I took to filling shoe boxes with the notebook pages and the random pieces of paper. On top, I'd pile the little black computer disks containing electronic manuscript drafts. Sometimes

I labeled the disks and sometimes I didn't. Sometimes I used them as coasters. Occasionally, Allison would add one to her preschool art, glitter, glue, beads, et cetera. Occasionally, a shoe box got misplaced or thrown out. I said it was a system. I did not say it was a good one.

Behind me is a vast closet, the kind you only find in the suburbs. I keep things in it that see little use. Snow pants, parkas so fluffy you can barely latch your seat belt when you have one on, cowboy boots that become fashionable every five to seven years. I roll my desk chair over and climb up. On the top shelf are a dozen shoe boxes. They're old. I can tell because I still wore a size seven shoe when I bought them, and I haven't worn a size seven shoe since before I was pregnant. I pull down the boxes and stack them on my desk.

I yank the lid off the box for a pair of floral stilettos I wore exactly once. Inside is a mess of paper and black disks. I remember reading Allison a Clifford the Big Red Dog book when she was a kid. In one scene Emily Elizabeth, the heroine, puts her tiny puppy, Clifford, on a turntable to give him a spin.

"What's that?" Allison asked, pointing to the record player. I ended up explaining all about defunct technology, right up through music CDs. We never finished the book.

The disks are like that. Defunct. Even if I find the one I'm looking for, my laptop will not be able to read it. The shred of hope I experienced earlier in the minivan, on the side of the road, is wholly tied to the paper notes, which look a lot like old confetti. My heart sinks. This is not going to work.

And pulling those spells, written twelve years ago, directly from memory is hardly even worth trying. I will only end up regurgitating bits of the Shakespearean sonnets my father drilled into me when I was a kid. And I don't need sonnets. I need spells.

I dig a hand into the box and pull out a notebook page. My handwriting is terrible. Do they even teach handwriting anymore, or is that as defunct as the disks and the turntable?

"Home Depot. The rope aisle. The yellow kind. Nylon. Do they do it in the bathroom over by the tractors?"

I have no idea what this note is about, but clearly my witches never went to Home Depot. I close the box and shove it aside. The next box is far more practical, for a pair of Birkenstocks I eventually wore out. They were patent leather, so I didn't come off as too hippie chick.

"Rain and wind like the scene in *Sense and Sensibility*. They race across a field into each other's arms at the end. Except she has a broken leg. Rework injury."

Not that one either. I move on to a pair of expensive Nike running shoes. This makes me smile. For about ten minutes on a spring Saturday, I was a runner. I wore the shoes to the supermarket for years however. I yank open the box.

"Evangeline younger, prettier, the wild sister? Clarissa a better witch."

I can tell from the slant of the writing that I jotted this down while driving. The last words go clear off the edge of the flyer that had been tucked under my windshield wiper, some-

thing about home delivery of dry cleaning. At least I have found the right box.

Before I can get too excited about its contents, the doorbell rings. Jason. My heart leaps at the sound. Quickly, I stuff everything back in the box and run downstairs, a little scared at how desperately I want to see him.

Chapter 27

Without asking, I put a bottle of chilled Chardonnay on the kitchen table between us. The bottle sweats. I pour two glasses and slide one in front of Jason. I hold the shoe box to my chest. Jason smiles.

"Where are your friends?" he asks.

"Upstairs," I say, nodding toward the ceiling. "Cleaning up after a gritty New York day. It was brutal out there today." In more ways than one.

"So how exactly do you know them?"

"Oh," I say. "Family friends from way back. Friends of my parents. The son of some friends of my parents. Younger friends." How much deeper can I dig this hole and still have any hope of getting out of it, I wonder.

"Well, I'm glad I have you to myself for a minute," he says. "Can you sit down?"

I realize I'm standing over him, glass of wine in hand. I do not want to sit. Sitting implies a serious conversation. But I do as I'm asked, putting the shoe box down by the wine. Jason takes my hands in his. He lets go. He drinks. His hands shake. He is definitely here to release me from our sexual contract. I'm consumed with sadness, and I haven't even heard what he has to say yet.

"So?" I say. Outside the window, I see Greta in the rose garden. She wears green gardening gloves and holds a pair of shears. Jason takes a deep breath. He rubs his palms together. He's nervous.

"I've been thinking a lot lately about our arrangement," he says finally.

Here it comes. I'm about to be fired.

"I told myself I would be honest in this relationship," he says. "I told myself I would not make the same mistakes twice. I'd say what I liked and didn't like. I'd be more assertive. You know. That stuff."

I nod. I focus on his face, but I feel worse than I have all day.

"I really like you, Sadie. Actually, it's more than really liking you. I think about you all the time. I imagine you with me. I see things and wonder what you'd say about them. I hear you laughing. I miss you six days out of seven. I know our arrangement is about sex, but I'm sorry, I can't help the way I feel. And more importantly, I don't want to. I don't even want to try."

I blush. A rosy, warm glow fills me in a way at once un-

familiar and comforting. I have been here before, haven't I? Or am I just remembering scenes I jotted down on scraps of paper? I put down my wineglass and take Jason's hands in mine. They're soft and able and weathered. They are not unlike mine. I put one to my cheek and hold it there, aware he's waiting for a response.

Before I answer, I want to take a moment and bask in this feeling. I want to explore its soft edges, its whispers, its racing heart. I want to remember how it can change my face, brighten the darkness behind my eyes. I want to remember it because as soon as I open my mouth, I'm going to blow it all to hell.

"I feel the same way," I say. And I do. The blush floods into the spaces I maintain between the disparate parts of myself— mother, writer, lover, breadwinner—and I feel myself momentarily whole. Fortunately, it will be so brief that later I will not recall its details or its depth.

Jason looks relieved. He runs his thumb down the curve of my cheek. I lean over the table, bumping the wineglasses, and kiss him. If this were my book, I'd have us go for it right here. Seal our mutual proclamations of "like" with some good old-fashioned fucking on the kitchen table. But this is not a novel. This is real life. And I must confess my sins, such as they are.

"I'm so glad," he says, pulling away. "So glad, Sadie. And it's not just sex. I mean, it was at first because that's why we got together, right? And I don't want to sound like the sex isn't good. It's great. I've never been with anyone like you. But I want to take you out and show you off to my friends. I want to meet your daughter. I want to be in your life and not just on Friday mornings. I'm rambling, I know, but I'm just glad, that's all."

Well, you might want to hold that thought, Jason.

"There's something I need to tell you," I say. For a woman whose stock-in-trade is words, I'm at a loss. How on earth do I explain this situation to a rational human being? A lawyer, no less?

"You can tell me anything, Sadie," he says. "I want that kind of relationship."

"Wait here," I say. "I need to get something." I run upstairs, grab my laptop, and race back to the kitchen. I shove the wineglasses aside and drop the machine on the table.

"Sadie?"

I flip it open. The manuscript for *Stolen Secrets* is just as I left it, complete with Clarissa and half a chapter I did not write. I'm about to launch into a summation of the whole mess when a thundering noise from above draws our attention. It sounds like bodies hitting the floor.

"What was that?" Jason asks. He's ready to jump into action and defend my honor from marauding intruders infiltrating from above.

"Don't worry," I say. "It's nothing." But I'm oddly tickled by his response. It's nice, romantic. The only time we encountered a mugger in Manhattan, Roger literally hid behind me. I was so busy pulling out wallets and watches and things to give the batshit crazy guy, I did not process Roger's reaction until later. And then I have to say it didn't surprise me much.

"It sounds like someone just fell out of bed," he says, still staring at the ceiling.

That could very well be true. If I had to guess, I would say my guests were having an athletic round of makeup sex, which can always be counted on for at least one good steamy chapter.

Chapter 28

Jason stares at the ceiling, his eyebrows furrowed.

"You're sure I shouldn't go up there and check it out?"

"No," I say. "Definitely don't do that. I want to read you something." He shakes his head, confused. He's trying to puzzle out how we got from talking about us and this new stage of our relationship to "Read Aloud with Sadie Fuller." Before he reconsiders his proclamation and runs away, I refill his glass and read him the three chapters of *Stolen Secrets*.

"It's good," Jason says when I finish. "Does your friend Aidan know he's starring in your book? Not that I can blame you exactly. He's perfect for it."

I clear my throat. My hands shake. I wait for panic to rear its ugly head, but it stays away.

"He actually came from the book," I say. "Or out of the book."

"It's very realistic," Jason agrees, missing the point. But perhaps that is because the point is completely absurd.

"No," I say slowly. "I wrote him and he *appeared*. In Target. And then I rescued him from the hospital. But the whole witch angle is not really my fault. I mean, I wrote Clarissa, but not for this novel, so I don't understand why she is after Aidan. And I didn't write the last bit I just read you. That part just appeared . . . somehow . . . on my laptop."

Jason pushes back from the table, putting space between us. This is the beginning of the end. But maybe he would have confessed to voting Republican and it wouldn't have worked out anyway. The edges of my heart start to crinkle up like Shrinky Dinks.

"Let me get this straight," Jason says in a tone I frequently used on Allison when she was a toddler. "You're telling me the characters from this half-written novel of yours have come to life? Like Frosty the Snowman?"

"Yes," I say, trying to avoid his incredulous expression. "Except I no longer control the story. Clarissa hijacked it from me. Are you following any of this?"

The silence that comes next is wide and deep, and I think I could actually disappear in it for quite some time. Jason sets his empty glass down. He folds his hands neatly in his lap, narrows his gaze, and watches me.

I go to the wine refrigerator and pull out another bottle, with a screw cap for convenience. I splash some into my glass. I pace the kitchen, my bare feet sticking to the tile. With nothing to lose, I go for broke.

"I have to send them back, Jason," I say. "And I think a spell will do it. But how does it work? How do *I* make it work? I need help."

Now if I were Jason, I would politely thank me for the wine and the several months of sex and get the hell out of the house immediately. Once in the car, I would offer up a prayer of thanks to whatever gods intervened on my behalf and allowed for a bloodless escape. I would not go back. Never. Ever. On some level, we all suspect crazy might be contagious.

But Jason is not me. He buys time by refilling his own wine-glass, going to the freezer and getting a few ice cubes. He sits back down and sips slowly, like he's having tea with the queen. His measured movements give no sign of what he's thinking. I stop pacing. I sit down. I wait.

After a minute he stands up again. I expect now he will run. But he doesn't head toward the exit. Instead, he strides out of the kitchen and toward the stairs. I scramble out of my seat and rush after him. He takes the steps two at a time and is on the upper landing before I can stop him.

"What are you doing?" I yell after him.

"Interviewing the witness," he says. The guest room door is locked, but it's a lazy lock. A push with your shoulder like you mean business and it will let you have your way. Jason slams it hard and fast, and it pops open.

"What the hell?" Aidan cries. This is followed by an indig-nant scream from Lily. I peer into the room. They are under the covers, and clothes are strewn about the room. So I was right about the makeup sex.

"Are you or are you not part of a fictional universe?" Jason demands. His question perfectly crystallizes how far from sense we've strayed, and I'm shocked he can even bear to ask it. Aidan looks to me for guidance. I nod my head. Go ahead. Answer the question.

"Yes," Aidan says. Lily looks away, eyes squeezed shut.

"And you were sent here by a witch named Clarissa as the manuscript suggests?"

"Yes," he says, pulling the sheet up to their chins. Without another word, Jason slams the door and stomps back down the stairs. I follow close at his heels. When he reaches the bottom step, he sits down, hard. He props his elbows on his knees and rests his head in his hands.

"I'm a lawyer, Sadie," he says without looking at me. I place a hand on his shoulder. He shrinks from my touch. I fold my hands back in my lap, feeling those crinkly edges around my heart grow ever more fragile.

"A lawyer's stock-in-trade is logic and the supporting evidence. You know those movies where an attorney gets up in court and gives a passionate speech on behalf of the wrongly accused defendant?"

"Yes."

"Well, that only happens in the movies! Mostly, we move contract paragraphs around like puzzle pieces and hope to slip in a few things that the other guy will miss."

He turns to me. His eyes blaze.

"It's not exciting, Sadie, but it's who I am."

I won't cry. Crying is not something I do unless I've severed a limb. Somehow I know if I start, I will never stop, and I cannot imagine getting through even a single day that way. But the pain welling up in my chest will be hard to keep down.

"Here's the thing though," Jason says, shaking his head, "and I can't believe I'm saying this, but even if you're crazy, which, based on recent evidence I think you must be, I don't care. I'm willing to go along with whatever elaborate game you're playing."

These words hang between us, turning the air suddenly sweet.

"What?" I say. I'm sure I've heard him incorrectly.

"I was married for a long time to a woman who didn't like me that much," he says. "When I thought about it, I didn't like her that much either. I have laughed more with you in the past few months than I did with her in our entire marriage. And it feels good, like I found something I didn't know was missing. You look at the world in a way that makes me feel lighter. So I don't care what you're doing. I can play along if you'll let me."

He takes my hands in his and pulls me down to sit beside him. I lean in and kiss him. He smells good, clean, like he took a shower before coming over.

"Sadie," he whispers into my hair, and I sense he's smiling.

Joy can be elusive. Sometimes to achieve it, you must step out onto the street, even if you know you might be run over by a bus.

"Take me with you," he says. "I want to go along." His words sound like a prayer, a mantra. They sound like something good.

Chapter 29

Wait a minute," Jason says, staring into my shoe box with horror. I'm starting to think Jason is the kind of person who would never store anything of value in an unlabeled shoe box for twelve years. Is our relationship already doomed? "Say that part again."

"I wrote Clarissa before," I repeat. "I thought I could write a paranormal romance, but it turned out I couldn't so I abandoned the whole project." I dump the shoe box out onto the table. "And I'm hoping something in here will make everything clear. Like if I could find the right spell or something."

"You don't remember them?"

I write four novels a year with at least several false starts thrown in there for good measure. I'm just as likely to remember all the kids in my kindergarten class.

"Do you remember every time you've gone to court?" I ask.

"Absolutely." Well, no surprise there.

Most people are good at suspending their disbelief for a few hours in a dark movie theater or for a few chapters before passing out at night. It is one of our primary pleasures in life. But I'm asking Jason for quite a bit more. I'm asking him to blur the line between fantasy and reality. I'm asking him to bungee-jump tied to a shoelace. Of course, it might work, but we also might end up a stain at the bottom of the canyon.

"I'm sorry," I say abruptly. "About all of this. It's a lot."

"Don't be," he says. "It's oddly . . . fun."

From his expression, I can tell Jason is beginning to understand that fun is not a luxury in life. It is necessary for our mental survival. He looks surprised.

"It's a strange word for it, isn't it?" he says.

"You may not think it's so fun when you meet Clarissa," I say.

"Tell me about her," he says, swirling the wine in his glass. "Tell me about Clarissa and the spells. Talk it through and we might find something."

My paranormal witch story is not unusual for being incomplete. There are dozens of unfinished manuscripts in my wake. Some are a page and a half long, others count in the hundreds. But all are beyond resurrection. Once I abandon an effort, I never go back. It's too much like revisiting a failed romance or a broken marriage, especially when you know nothing can be gained from it.

Yet I've often wondered about the characters suspended in

midformation, with a beginning and possibly a middle but no end. Sometimes at night, when I've accepted a project is not going to work, I swear I can hear them begging me to push forward. Save us, they scream. Don't leave us here in limbo forever. Don't leave us incomplete. It's a little scary to think maybe they really have been speaking to me, that I've been sharing space with any number of pissed-off, half-baked characters.

I shudder at the thought. But Jason asked about Clarissa. I dig into the notes, spreading them out before us and forcing myself back over a decade. And this is what I tell him.

Clarissa Barnes was 212 years old but didn't look a day over 25, one of the upsides of being a witch. Over the long course of her life, she'd acquired substantial wealth by marrying rich men and waiting around until they died. There was one not particularly nice gentleman who required a bit of help getting to the end, but she never lost any sleep over it.

Clarissa lived with her sister, Evangeline Barnes. Evangeline was only 208 years old and took every opportunity to rub Clarissa's nose in it. But even so, both sisters knew Clarissa was the more powerful one. She had honed her craft over the centuries, and there was little she could not now command with a simple spell or charm.

One of the potential side effects of being old and powerful was boredom. It became harder and harder for the sisters to find ways to entertain themselves. Sure, they'd do the occasional haunting and enjoyed the screaming and terror of their victims well enough, but the high didn't last. By the next day they were back to gazing into crystal balls and messing with the weather in Florida.

One day, Clarissa was staring out the enormous picture window that fronted their East Sixty-Third Street mansion when she caught sight of a man. He was young, with wide shoulders tapering down to a narrow waist. Wearing the traditional blue of a New York City beat cop, he looked like a poster child for law enforcement. Standing on the sidewalk staring up at her house, he removed his hat and ran his fingers through his dark, thick hair. He twirled a bunch of strands around a forefinger in a way that appeared almost nervous. As he did so, Clarissa caught a glimpse of a thin, faint scar on his forehead from some long-ago trauma. The sun glinted off his aviator sunglasses so sharply, Clarissa had to look away.

Rubbing her eyes to erase the sun spots, she turned back to find the young man gesturing for her to come to the door. The sisters tried very hard to fly under the radar, so when a cop beckoned, Clarissa came. But not without some trepidation. There was something in this man's manner, as if he were quietly smoldering, simply waiting for a chance to pounce on an innocent young girl. Clarissa's heart danced in tight, dizzy circles. He made her mouth water.

"Excuse me, ma'am," the cop said as Clarissa threw open the heavy wooden front door. He removed his sunglasses and gave her a wicked smile, the kind that made clear he was well aware of his effect on women. He would not be a beat cop for long. As he stepped closer, Clarissa noticed how sharp his green eyes

were against his pale, clear skin. The combination threw her off balance. She steadied herself against the doorjamb.

"I'm sorry to trouble you," the cop said. "But I was walking by and I noticed your window there is slightly open." He gestured to one of the enormous street-level windows that was, in fact, wide open. "You might want to close it. Just to be on the safe side."

Evangeline liked to paint in the front room and often kept the window open to avoid asphyxiation from the oil paint fumes. She did primarily landscapes of hell, or at least how she envisioned hell to be. Clarissa found the paintings dreadful, but they sold quite well to the nouveaux riches in the West Village.

"Ah," Clarissa said. "My sister's rather forgetful. I'll close it right away. Thank you for noticing."

"Well, you can't be too careful, right? Who knows what sorts of characters might be lurking around these parts?" The beat cop laughed.

"True," Clarissa agreed. "You never can tell."

"Well, good day to you, ma'am," the cop said, and donned his cap once more.

Oh, but he could not leave! Not yet! She found herself longing for his company in a visceral, unfamiliar way. She wanted to gaze deep into his eyes and see what made him burn. Was it desire or power? Who *was* this man?

Evangeline fell in love every twenty years or so. It was always sticky, loud, and messy, and inevitably would reach a point where Clarissa would have to whip up a few spells to banish all involved parties to various realities just so she could get some rest. Afterward, Evangeline was always genuinely sorry for the trouble, but then a couple of decades would pass and she'd be right back at it.

"You don't understand love," she'd moan when Clarissa reminded her of how badly it always turned out. "The way I feel when I'm in a lover's arms, the anticipation, the need. It's unlike anything in this world!"

But Clarissa did understand love. She had been observing its effects for over two centuries. It made one vulnerable and weak. It made one stupid and careless. More often than not, instead of making a girl whole, it would rip her to shreds. It was a fool's game. And Clarissa was not a fool.

But right now she did not feel at all herself. She smiled down at the policeman.

"Do come in for coffee," she said. "Let me reward you for your vigilance."

"Thanks for the offer, ma'am," he said, "but I'm on duty."

Sparks of flower
Beware my heart
Change the power
And let it . . . start.

Clarissa chanted so quietly the cop was not even aware her lips were moving. He looked confused, as if time had somehow jumped forward and he had missed it.

"Did you say coffee?" he asked.

"Please," Clarissa said, stepping aside. "Come in and join me."

"Well, I guess it would be okay," he said, appearing slightly stunned. "Just for a minute. Chief says to get to know the people in the neighborhood."

"See?" Clarissa said. She swung the heavy door closed with a thud that made the man jump. "Just following orders. You're good at your job. I can tell. May I take your hat?"

His name was Officer Perkins. He was twenty-five. He had big hands and teeth that would make an orthodontist swoon. His broad chest filled his uniform, straining the gold-colored buttons that ran down the front. He sat across from Clarissa, smiling and sipping a cup of coffee literally conjured from midair. Of course, the conjuring was done while Officer Perkins's back was turned so as not to send the guy straight off the deep end first thing.

They chatted amiably about the neighborhood, but the air around them crackled with tension. After all, they *were* two beautiful people sharing a small space. By the time Clarissa escorted Officer Perkins to the door, the nugget of a rather evil plan had already begun to form in her mind.

"Evangeline, come here at once!"

Evangeline immediately materialized at Clarissa's elbow, almost as if she'd been around the corner watching.

"My darling sister, whatever can be making you bellow so?"

Clarissa grasped Evangeline's hands in her own and gave her a mischievous grin. Or it would have been mischievous on the face of a young child. On Clarissa, it was just plain nasty.

"I think I've found our entertainment for the next few months."

"Oh, do tell, dear sister. I've been so utterly bored I've taken to playing the stock market."

"I just met a man," Clarissa said. "A policeman. Young, attractive, possibly capable of human-style darkness. In any case, he was concerned our window was left open."

"Go on," Evangeline urged.

"I propose a challenge," Clarissa said, "a little friendly competition."

Evangeline frowned. "You remember what happened the last time we did that?"

Clarissa brushed off the question. "That was an accident. I think we both learned a lesson, don't you?"

Evangeline shrugged. "I suppose so. Certainly I can afford to hear you out."

"His heart," Clarissa said bluntly. "Who can win his heart?"

"That's it? *That's* the contest? The heart of a mortal man?"

Clarissa nodded.

"My word, dear sister, you're taking witchiness to the next level. Brilliant! A love test! And when the competition is complete?"

"The winner may do with Officer Perkins as she pleases."

"Oh, darling Clarissa!" Evangeline threw her arms around her sister's neck. "I accept. The game is on!"

And so it began, the quest to make Officer Perkins fall in love with one or the other of the Barnes sisters. They pulled

out all the stops. Potions, spells, chants, incantations. They went kinky, ingenue, innocent schoolgirl, and whore. There were no boundaries, nothing they would not try, And, as you might imagine, Officer Perkins enjoyed this aspect of the game he did not know he was playing immensely and decided not to examine the situation too closely for fear it would change. So the game went along just fine and everyone was truly entertained, although in different ways, until Evangeline actually began to fall in love with him. That, of course, complicated things.

At first, Clarissa could not see what was happening. Witches did not fall in love with humans. They stuck with their own kind and had, for as long as time had existed. So Evangeline harboring feelings for this mere mortal was preposterous. But all the signs were there. She walked around with an absentminded smile on her face. She couldn't eat. She sighed continuously, often interrupting Clarissa's train of thought. She would disappear for hours on end, only to return mysteriously, offering no information as to her whereabouts. She started to paint perfectly benign landscapes.

It was not Clarissa's fault she didn't figure it out sooner. After all, it had been about twenty-five years since Evangeline's last disastrous affair, and Clarissa had worked very hard to put that one out of her mind. After consulting the stars, Clarissa knew she had no choice but to confront her sister and end the game. It was no longer fun. It had become dangerous.

Clarissa was waiting in the parlor, a small fire burning in the grate, when Evangeline floated in one of the back doors. She barely noticed Clarissa as she passed, murmuring what sounded like the love spells a teenage witch might come up with.

"You cannot have him, you know," Clarissa said. Her voice stopped Evangeline in her tracks. The sisters stared at each other in the dim, flickering light. "He's a mortal man. You cannot cross over. It would be the end of you."

"My dear sister," Evangeline said after a moment. "How kind of you to wait up for me. And thank you for your concern about my well-being."

"The game is over," Clarissa said. "You must let him go."

Evangeline inhaled sharply, her angular features contorted.

"Why?" she asked. "So that you may have him for yourself? That's what you want, isn't it?"

Clarissa reeled back. How dare Evangeline suggest such a thing? But her sister just kept going.

"You love him," Evangeline hissed. "You have from the very day you suggested this game. I can see it on your face. But it's too late. He loves me. He's said as much!"

Clarissa howled in fury. The walls of the house shook. Evangeline was right. About *everything*.

Chapter 30

J ason sits on the edge of his chair, his lips parted ever so slightly.

"Well?" he asks, eyes wide.

"Well what?" I say. I've sorted my notes into little piles, arranged by size. Not the most efficient approach, but at least they look tidy now.

"What *happened*?" Jason shouts. "What happened to the sisters?"

"I don't know," I say. "I never finished."

"Why didn't you finish?"

"I didn't know what to do next," I say. "Plus I think I met Roger in there somewhere and got pregnant with Allison, and, you know, I got distracted. Plus paranormal isn't easy. I know. I tried."

"Is this going to happen a lot?" Jason asks, leaning back in the chair and wiping his sweaty forehead on his shirtsleeve. He could be talking about so many different things I'm actually afraid to answer. "Because I'm not sure I can take it. Stories without endings, without resolutions. It might drive me crazy."

"Do you finish every book you start?" I ask.

"Always," he says.

It's funny how when a relationship seems to have long-term prospects, you examine the details through a different lens. When Jason was simply my Friday morning lay, I did not care if he finished his books or remembered every detail of every event in his life. But now I do.

And I just don't have the heart to tell him I can come up with a new concept for a novel while standing on line at the grocery store and have already discarded it as shit by the time my items are bagged up and ready to go. This happens a lot. When it finally stops happening, that will be the day I become a CPA or a personal trainer.

"You don't?" Jason asks.

I shake my head. If a novel hasn't grabbed me in the first fifty pages, I move on. I'm getting older every day. I have no time to waste on books I don't like.

"Not always," I say.

"Okay," Jason says, shaking off this conversational thread like a dog does water. He flips through a small notebook he has taken from his pocket. He runs his finger down the page.

"You took notes?" I ask.

"The win is in the details," he says. He'd make a fine editor if he ever grows bored with the law. "The cop, Perkins, he twirls his hair?"

"Yes," I say. I take a piece of my own frizzy mop and demonstrate.

"And he has a scar?"

I nod, my eyes fixed on him as if he is going to reveal the secrets of the universe any minute now.

"And he"—Jason pauses—"smolders? Is that the word?"

Yes. Taken out of context, many of the best erotic descriptors sound funny. But Jason doesn't laugh.

"Sadie?" he asks.

"Jason?"

"Are you *still* not thinking what I'm thinking?"

"I don't know. Am I?"

A flash of exasperation. "The man in your guest room," he says. "Coincidence, or do you just like them that way?"

No. I like them like you. Just like you. And, more important, there cannot be any coincidences. If there are, your plot has holes big enough to swallow your story. I want to leap across the table and hug Jason because he's detail oriented and nice and all of a sudden, pretty hot, and not because of the weather.

"Aidan is recycled too," I say, breathless. "He's the cop!"

Jason gives me an exaggerated head nod. "Sure sounds like it to me," he says.

I'm amazed a manuscript I abandoned without a thought has clung so tightly to me for so many years.

"Clarissa is here to reclaim the cop she lost to Evangeline." I speak rapidly. I'm a little afraid of myself. "She thinks he belongs to her, but she has to get Lily out of the picture and out of his system. Is that right?"

"Could be," Jason says.

"Oh my god, Jason," I say. "So now what?" My hands shake. I feel weak. And here I thought recycling was supposed to be good for you.

"We still need the spell," Jason says. "If we can send them back, their story has a chance of being finished as you intended, without Clarissa."

And maybe the happily ever after is not a total loss.

Jason plucks a Chinese take-out menu from the pile of notes and reads the words I squeezed between the wonton soup and the egg rolls.

So, till the judgment that yourself arise,
You live in this, and dwell in lovers' eyes.

"That's good," Jason says.

"That's Shakespeare," I say. To this day, writing bits of Shakespeare or 1980s song lyrics is my way of doodling.

"Oh," Jason says. "Okay. Moving on." I adore him so completely at this moment, I feel almost drunk. Although judging by the empty bottles, actually being drunk is a distinct possibility.

Working our way through the notes, we find seven possibilities. I finally settle on the one that seems most likely

to have cast lovers into a cold and unwelcoming alternative universe.

> *Be not afraid of what draws near,*
> *Lady Love is wicked, as you know,*
> *And now she takes you, just as you are,*
> *To a distant and unfamiliar shore.*

Jason stops, pen poised above his notebook, and looks up.

"Shakespeare was the master," I say in self-defense.

"It's not bad," Jason says.

"It's not good either," I say.

"But it doesn't matter," he says with complete confidence. "Because it's the one."

"How do you know? What if it's the wrong one?" I ask. "What if it doesn't work? What if it makes things worse? What if we all disappear?"

Jason clicks his pen closed and slides both it and the notebook into his pocket. He smiles.

"Do you trust me?" he asks.

I do. Absolutely and completely. What a strange experience.

"Yes," I say.

"Then there's only one way to find out," he says.

I was afraid he was going to say that.

Jason stands, takes my hand. and pulls me toward the stairs. On our way to the guest room, we make as much noise as possible in the hope that Aidan and Lily will hear us coming, get dressed, and sit on opposite sides of the room.

This time, I knock.

"Hello in there," I say. I sound ridiculous. Jason hides a smile. I punch him in the biceps. "You're not helping."

"Yes?"

"Aidan," I say. "It's Sadie. Can I come in?"

There's shuffling, murmuring from inside.

"One minute," he says.

When he finally opens the door, he's moderately disheveled, his hair tousled just so, his shirt inside out. His eyes gleam, and his lips are slightly swollen, probably from all that mashing. I blush, suddenly wishing my imagination were a little less vivid. Behind him, Lily sits on the edge of the bed. She's back in the orange dress, running her fingers through her hair. There's a hairbrush in the guest bathroom, brand-new and wrapped in plastic to prove it because that is the way Greta rolls. I'm about to mention it to Lily when I reconsider. This situation is awkward enough.

"Sorry to interrupt," I say. Jason appears next to me. He peers into the bedroom.

"Aidan," I say, "this is my friend Jason. You guys met last night at the fund-raiser. He's a lawyer. I thought he might help us sort through this situation."

"Wasn't he with your neighbor?" Aidan eyes Jason but speaks to me.

"Yes," I say. "They were on a date."

"But he's with you?"

"Yes."

"You're complicated, Sadie," Aidan says.

"Only after you showed up," I shoot back.

"Nice to see you again, Aidan," Jason interrupts. "Sorry about barging in on you earlier."

"And that's Lily back there," I say. Lily half-waves but continues running her fingers through her snarled red curls. If you want to know if someone just had sex, look at the hair. It doesn't matter if you do it standing up, afterward, the hair is always a mess.

"So?" Aidan asks. He acts as if I'm intruding.

"I found a spell," I say. "I want to try it."

Lily leaps from the bed and runs to us.

"To send us back?" she asks, eyes blazing.

"Yes," I say. I think so. I hope so. But really I have no idea.

Aidan opens the door. "Please come in," he says.

Jason and I squeeze into the small bedroom. It smells of lust and sweat, and my armpits immediately go damp. There are too many of us. Jason retreats to a corner. Lily sits on the bed, Aidan beside her. I stand front and center, feeling exactly how Professor Marvel, the mysterious traveling fortune-teller, must have in *The Wonderful Wizard of Oz*. Totally full of shit.

"How do we do it?" Aidan asks.

"I don't know," I say. "Maybe you guys hold hands and I say the spell?"

"Are you serious?" Lily asks.

"If you have a better idea, I'd love to hear it," I say. She's awfully tense for a woman who just had a roll in the hay. I'd hate to see her after a few months of celibacy.

"No," she says. "I just thought there'd be more ritual or something."

I'm sure there is. I'm sure I'd do better if I had a magic wand or a fancy hat or any clue what I was doing. But I don't.

"Hold hands," I say. I wave my arms around in front of me for good measure. I am sure I look ridiculous. "Be not afraid of what draws near, Lady Love is wicked, as you know, And now she takes you, just as you are, To a distant and unfamiliar shore."

I close my eyes. I fill my mind with a haze of purple smoke. I wait. Nothing happens.

"That was the spell?" Lily stares at me, incredulous. "It sounds like it was written by a fifth grader."

"I'm not Shakespeare!" I shout.

Jason slides his hands over my shoulders.

"Let's try again," he suggests. "This time, Aidan, you say the words, okay?"

Aidan nods. I think he'd don a gorilla suit and dance a jig in Grand Central Terminal if I told him it might get him out of here. The two sit back on the bed and take each other's hands.

"Close your eyes," Jason says. He sounds so confident, so authoritative, like he knows what he's doing. I find it incredibly

sexy. "Now, say the words. Whisper them and don't stop until I say to."

Aidan does as he's told. I can barely hear him, but I see my silly verse falling from his lips. He and Lily hold hands so tightly their knuckles turn white. Jason watches them closely. His fingers dig into my shoulders. He's nervous, captivated.

A pale yellow light fills the room. It's soft and warm, like concentrated sunshine. The dust is iridescent in its glow.

"Don't stop," Jason whispers. "Keep going."

The air grows thicker. Aidan and Lily keep their eyes shut tight. Jason and I step back so we are flat against the wall.

The image is faint, floating in the middle of the room as if projected from a camera mounted on the ceiling. It's Clarissa, still dressed all in black. She holds something in her hands that is not quite clear, and she laughs, the same agonizing cackle we heard from her in the park. It's an awful sound, and I instinctively raise my hands to my ears.

"Sadie?" Jason asks.

Yes. I nod. This is Clarissa.

"Wow," he says. Indeed. *Wow* is one word for it.

"I know they're hiding," the ghostly Clarissa says. "I know they think they can figure out how to get back and live happily ever after. But don't they know? There is *no* happily ever after. Not for them. Not for anybody."

My back is pressed so tight against the wall I fear I may push right through it and end up falling two stories into the garden.

Aidan and Lily remain on the bed, unaware of the apparition in the room with us.

Clarissa turns slowly, spinning above the floor. I cannot tell if she can see us or if this is a one-way mirror.

"Excuse me," Jason says quietly. "Can you hear me?"

"Yes," I say. "I'm standing right here."

"Not you, Sadie," he says. "That." He points at Clarissa. She does not respond to his question, but she turns in my direction.

Our eyes don't meet because she gazes at a point well beyond me.

"There is so little time left," she says, almost thoughtfully. "And I want to be there to claim my prize when the clock runs out." At her words, my stomach clenches, and daggers of pain spiral down my legs. Clarissa gives a wicked smile as if she can see my agony painted in bright colors across the room. She takes a step forward, right to the edge of the projection that contains her, and holds up the item in her hands.

It's a hardcover novel. I recognize it instantly. It's one of my recent Sadie Fuller romances, about a cowboy and a city girl who, against all odds, fall in love. Clarissa caresses the book. It's as if her hands are on me. She starts to laugh again.

I fall to my knees, consumed by blackness.

Chapter 31

S adie. Sadie! Open your eyes." Jason's voice drifts toward me over what feels like a great distance. I struggle to focus, but my head hurts. When I finally will my eyes to open, I find three faces staring down at me, a deep look of concern etched on at least one of them.

"What happened?" I ask. I try to sit up, but I'm dizzy. Jason eases me onto his lap.

"Do you remember?"

A sudden surge of bile in my mouth indicates that yes, I do remember.

"The cowboy book," I whisper. It's not my favorite, but it's sold well. Romance reviewers claimed I took a cliché and made it fresh. I wanted to send each and every one of them a bottle of champagne, because deep down, I was worried it was just about as fresh as three-day-old kitty litter.

"Yes," Jason says. He has a strange look on his face, part shock, part amusement.

"So she knows where I live," I say, flatly. "It's on the book jacket." I guess the last time Clarissa and I crossed paths I still lived in New York City. It did not take her very long to figure out I'd moved.

"And your spell didn't work," Lily sniffs, sitting back on her heels.

"Well," Jason says. "It worked. It just didn't work as we intended it to work."

"But now we know she's coming here," Aidan says. He's ragged, his face pale. If I could see into him, I'd see his heart racing, consumed by the anxiety of powerlessness.

"She wouldn't miss the end," I agree. "That's the best part."

"This is ridiculous," Lily wails. "I just want to go home. I want to sit on my couch and watch TV. I want to drink a latte, look out the window and see *my* reality. Is that so much to ask? Do you have any more spells we could try?"

Aidan puts a comforting arm around her. She pushes him away. I'm beginning to wonder what he sees in this girl.

"I thought this one was it," I say. "We must be missing something. A clue. We just need to be smarter." And we need to do it fast because the witch is on her way.

I try to get to my feet. I sway. I stagger. Jason props me up. I loop my arm through his and hang on. The sound of a throat

clearing draws my attention to the door. There stands Greta. Her hands are on her hips, and she taps one leather loafer.

"Greta," I say, attempting a normal smile.

"I heard a noise," she says, "from outside." I must have made quite a thump when I hit the floor for her to hear me in the rose garden. "Is everything okay?"

"Yes," I say with a smile that hurts my face.

Greta flicks an invisible bit of dust from her sleeve. "I'm preparing cold ham and pasta salad for dinner," she says. We are hot and disheveled, and there is a good bit of unspoken dialogue occurring in the room. I'm sure right now Greta is wondering why she decided to throw in with me all those years ago. She turns and leaves without another word. In twenty minutes, she will have dinner made and the table set. There will be wine and linen napkins. And she will not ask us what the hell is going on. Ever.

"Get the laptop from downstairs," I tell Jason. "Meet us back in my office." I can't stand to be in this guest room for another second.

The three of us enter my office. My sanctuary. It's painted pale green, and the walls are decorated with poster advertisements for my various books. The shelves overflow with my favorite novels, those I can't bear to live without. I tend not to reread things, but I like the security of knowing I can if I want to. This is where I come to be myself, as authentic a self as I am likely to achieve.

Jason places my laptop on my desk. I sit in front of it. I

scroll back through the passages I did not write. I read the part where Clarissa offers Aidan the deal outside the restaurant.

> "I'll give you forty-eight hours to find your Lily and figure out the magic that will get you two back here. If you succeed, you get your Lily and my life. But if you fail, I own you forever. Will you accept my terms?"

The room is still. They all stare at me.

"The magic words," Aidan says finally. "A spell. We already knew that."

But that is not exactly what it says. It says "magic."

"We might be misreading," I say.

"Sadie," Jason says. "It *has* to be a spell. That's the only possibility we have of figuring out the riddle. If it's just a bunch of random words or actions, we're screwed."

He's right. An unsolvable mystery would never make it past a good editor. I sigh. This is worse than writer's block. But then Lily speaks up.

"Maybe Sadie's onto something," she says, crossing her arms against her chest and spreading her feet as if she is preparing for a physical blow. "Maybe magic means something else."

Her voice is not exactly like that of the woman I trailed out of Grand Central on a day that seems to belong to another lifetime. It's a bit higher and certainly more steely. My Grand Central gal had a lilt. Her voice was melodious and I could see her using it to great effect lulling a fussy baby to sleep at some point in her unknown future. The Lily standing in front of me owns her voice. It belongs only to her.

The rules say that the reader must identify with the romantic heroine. The story does not belong to the hero. He is simply a vessel by which the heroine can reach her full potential and her joy. She is the focus.

I've been approaching this situation from Aidan's perspective because he showed up first and I think I like him more. But there is no doubt *Stolen Secrets* is Lily's story, told in her voice. She is the driving force.

"Lily," I say. "This may sound weird, but you need to tell us about yourself."

"What?"

"Backstory," I say. "Maybe what we're looking for is in there somewhere." Yes, I should know her history inside and out, but I'm afraid since her arrival here it has changed in ways I can no longer see. Will the magic we are trying to find reveal itself if we take a closer look? It's worth a try.

"I hate talking about myself," she says.

"Please," I say. "Can you try?"

"If you think it will help," she says. I don't know if it will, but I'm running out of ideas.

"It might," I say.

With a shrug, she gives us her story.

Lily was raised down south, in a lonely and run-down suburb of Memphis. She lived in a small ranch house that was always in a state of disrepair. The screens had holes in them and the front door creaked loudly on its hinges. In the winter, she had to sleep in her cheap down jacket, otherwise she ran the risk of freezing to death during the night. There was never any money for heating oil. There was never any money for anything.

Lily never knew her father.

"Love will just break your heart, Lily. Don't do it if you don't got to." And that was all her mother, Gloria, would say on the subject of her father.

During the day, Gloria worked in the plumbing department of Home Depot. She knew her shit and she looked hot in the uniform, so the plumbing department never seemed devoid of customers. Men would come in and buy just a little of this or a little of that so they could spend time with her.

At night, she worked as a cocktail waitress at a local roadside bar. She wore short skirts and low-cut shirts and did pretty well when it came to tips. But as her loveliness faded so did the tips. Times were hard.

Occasionally, Gloria would bring a man home from the bar. She never brought home a customer from the Home Depot. The Depot was serious business. The Depot was health insurance and a steady, if small, paycheck. The Depot was their lifeline, a fact of which Gloria was all too aware.

The men from the bar smelled of whiskey and cigarettes, and would disappear with Gloria into her tiny bedroom. Lily would hear giggles and moans through the paper-thin walls and would don her cheap headphones to cancel out the sounds. On

her bed, with music blasting, she'd work her algebra sets or read her history textbook while her mother had sex with a stranger not ten feet away.

But it was okay, Lily thought. The guy, whoever he was, would always be gone by morning and Gloria, dressed for another day in plumbing supplies, would be at the electric stove frying eggs for Lily's breakfast.

But while Gloria accepted her life, she had another one in mind for Lily, one that went beyond roadside bars and DIY superstores. She would launch her beautiful daughter out of this hellhole no matter what it took. She was strict about schoolwork and bedtimes and forced Lily to participate in any number of after-school activities to keep her busy and out of trouble. She lectured her on the dangers of boyfriends and sex and drugs. The focus was on the future. The present was simply a step on the way. Gloria's only child would go to college or Gloria would die trying to get her there.

And Lily was a natural. Beautiful, smart, and able, she coasted through high school, heeding her mother's advice, getting good grades, and making an impression on the dilapidated tennis courts that ran alongside a municipal park in town.

She attended the University of Wisconsin on scholarship and worked three jobs to make ends meet. She ate ramen noodles twice a day, bargained for used textbooks, and walked everywhere, even in the blinding snow. After graduating at the top in her class, she made a beeline for New York City and never looked back.

When Lily was growing up, Gloria always made it clear that men served only to sidetrack women from their goals.

"Men come along, get you knocked up, and leave," she used to say. "Then you got a kid to feed, and everything you thought you were, none of that matters anymore."

So Lily carried with her a wariness of men and their intentions. She focused on her career, thinking success had to feel at least as good as sex and was much less risky. The first time she experienced the hot little fingers of lust was in the elevator with Aidan Hathaway.

Chapter 32

We sit around my big dining room table, listening to the end of Lily's tale. We are certainly the world's strangest impromptu dinner party, but even made-up people need to eat. Greta has propped a fan in the corner that blows the lacy edges of the curtains in a continuous loopy pattern. The old grandfather clock indicates the passing quarter hours with sharp chimes. Every lost fifteen minutes feels like a poke in the eye.

In the beginning of *Stolen Secrets,* at least the parts I wrote, Lily diligently followed the pattern of a leading lady. She appeared to be governed by the rules of erotic romance. When I asked for her backstory, I thought something in it might trigger an understanding of the magic Clarissa says we need. But the Lily sitting beside me now is so different from the one on the page that her past almost requires reinterpretation. It was designed to make her vulnerable to men like Aidan Hathaway, but in this reality, it made her tough. It made her strong and ready, even if she does not know what for. I wrote one thing and Lily made it another.

She looks at me expectantly.

"So?" she says. "Anything."

I shake my head. "No," I say. "Sorry. We're no closer."

My companions take that one hard. We are a forlorn group, out of ideas, watching the clock, waiting for the show's finale.

I don't want to look at anyone. I run my fingers along the tablecloth. It belonged to my grandmother, who was dead by the time I was born, but I cherish the link the cloth provides. There's comfort in knowing what came before me. And in popular culture there's not much of that. A minute can be a lifetime. Everything is disposable, from the books we read to the cars we drive to the clothes we wear.

Even love is disposable these days. We treat it poorly, it dies, and we move on. Or it never shows up to begin with because our expectations are out of line with reality. We spend too much time wallowing in the happily-ever-afters of fictitious characters rather than going out and creating our own.

Happily ever after. The words echo in my head. Of course! Just because this story has jumped the page does not mean it can escape the most fundamental rule of romance. I leap from my seat.

"Happily ever after," I say. "The rules according to Ellen. Eyes for each other only and for always." I narrow my gaze on Aidan and Lily.

"The magic is love," I say. "Saying 'I love you'!"

More powerful than any spell, more binding than time, love is the most dynamic force in our universe. It can even withstand death.

"Hasn't anyone at this table read *Wuthering Heights*?" I ask.

There are defensive murmurs all around.

"I guess not," I say. "Lily and Aidan, you've both changed. Clarissa's bet banked on you two remeeting in this reality and not liking each other, but she was wrong. Aidan, you can love a strong, independent woman, and Lily, you can love a man like . . . Aidan. Right?"

"So what does that mean in practice?" Jason asks. Men, even the good ones, are all the same in certain situations.

"A declaration of love," I say impatiently. "You two say it to each other, and bam, I bet you're home in time for breakfast." I smile. I'm proud of myself. I feel good all over.

"Is there a catch?" Aidan asks.

"Well, you have to mean it," I say. False declarations of love do not magic make. I turn to Lily to see how she's taking the news. Her skin is chalky, her eyes wide. She swallows repeatedly like the small amount of dinner she's had time to consume is crawling back up her throat. It's not quite the reaction I expected.

"Is that the only way?" she asks. The question is directed at me. Aidan takes her hands in his.

"This sounds right, Sadie," Aidan says. He's excited. For the first time since he arrived here, he looks hopeful. "I think we're going to be okay."

Lily gives him a wan smile.

"Sadie!" Greta yells from the kitchen. "Please come in here."

I share Aidan's excitement. I believe I've got it figured out.

"Be right back," I say. "No one go anywhere." I race out of the dining room and into the kitchen.

"What do you need?" I ask Greta.

"Nothing."

I pause.

"But you called me."

"Yes."

"So?"

She makes a twirling motion with her fingers, indicating I should turn around. When I do, I bump right into Lily, who has followed me into the kitchen.

"I need to talk to you," Lily says. I sometimes wonder if Greta is the truly magical one among us. She knows things. I have no idea how, but she does.

"Sure," I say.

"I can't do it," she says bluntly.

"What?" I ask. "Go back? Of course you can. You'll get your happy ending and everything."

"No," she says, shaking her head. "I can't tell Aidan I love him."

"Why?" I ask. "You don't have to be scared. He loves you for who you are. This man isn't going to break your heart. I promise."

"No, Sadie," she says. "You're not listening to me."

There are shades of Allison in those words.

"Okay," I say. "Explain." Behind me, Greta studies her cookbook, but I'm keenly aware of her presence. *She's* listening. She is not missing the point.

"I can't tell Aidan I love him," Lily says, "because I don't love him."

Her words make me instantly dizzy. I lean on the kitchen island. This is not how I imagined this scene progressing.

"But," I say, "that's the reason you exist, even if you have changed a little. To fall in love with a beautiful man and drive off into the sunset. In a fancy car. Wearing nice clothes. And impractical shoes."

Lily holds up a hand for me to stop.

"This is your house, right?" she asks.

"Yes."

"You bought it, you paid for it. You work for yourself. You decide what to have for breakfast, what clothes to put on. You choose what channel to watch."

"Not always," I say. "I have an eleven-year-old daughter."

"You know what I mean," Lily says.

I look down at my feet. I do not like where this is going.

"And you have Jason," she says. "I bet you guys talk about things. I bet you laugh together. I'm sure he doesn't treat you like a delicate flower always at risk of wilting in the heat."

Definitely no delicate flower issues.

"And I bet when you got divorced from Roger, you dated a bunch of men. You dated anyone you wanted. You got to decide."

I want to clarify for her just how awesome the dating thing turned out for me, but that's not her point.

"Yes," I say. "To all those things."

"Well," Lily says, taking a step closer. Even in bare feet she towers over me. "I want all that. I want to be in charge of my own life. I don't want to be arm candy for some superrich, incredibly good-looking guy."

"But don't you like Aidan?" I sputter. "He's nice . . . and good looking . . . and things. I know he may appear shallow to you now, but he'll get better. I swear." It's the rules.

"I do like him," she says. "I don't love him."

I sink into a chair beside Greta.

"Trouble," Greta says, without looking up.

I'll say. There's no point in asking Lily to fake it. It won't work. It might even backfire. I lay my head down on my arms.

"Can you help me explain this to Aidan?" Lily asks quietly.

No. No. No. One hundred times, no.

"Yes," I say.

Lily's story is not done. I can see her with a short, geeky guy who creates video games for a living. I can see her with an older professorial type. I can see her with a professional athlete who likes to get up at dawn to run laps around an empty Central Park. I can see her having children and going back to work. I can see her discovering all on her own how difficult it is to have everything you think you want.

These opportunities for exploration, for finding one's path, stumbling, finding it again, are the moments that make us who

we are. It is all I want for my daughter, to be bold enough to go where she wants to, to be unafraid of the world around her. Is it fair that I would want less for my leading lady?

"You belong in a different book," I mutter. "You belong on the women's fiction shelves. Not erotic romance." Of course, over on the women's fiction shelves, we would not be in danger of Lily disappearing into thin air in under an hour. Or of her being banished to another dimension for all eternity. That doesn't happen in women's fiction.

"Sorry," Lily says.

"Never mind," I say. Now is probably not the best time for a discussion of genre fiction versus general fiction. "We should go back in there and see what we can make of all this."

I'm about to return to the dining room when Greta grabs my arm. She has a surprisingly strong grip, and I lurch to a halt.

"This is a house of women," she says, matter-of-fact. "Room can be made." Before I ask her why she has chosen now to begin speaking in code, she releases me and returns to her study of beef bourguignon. Greta and I don't hug or touch, but after a decade I can read her body language almost perfectly. Her posture says, "Don't ask me anything." It says "go away."

So I do. But I can't help thinking Greta just suggested we *keep* Lily here. In our house. In our reality.

Chapter 33

When I invented K. T. Briggs, I had to create a biography to go with her. In the old days, which means a time before the Internet, writing under a pseudonym was no big deal. A short paragraph on the book jacket was all that was required. It could be as brief as "The author lives in San Francisco with her golden retriever and a small green parrot." It was rare for a reader to spend her valuable time investigating whether the author really *did* live in San Francisco with the dog and the bird or whether it was a ruse and she *really* lived in Texas with a husband and four kids. I mean, at the end of the day, who cares?

But in a world driven by social media, things are more complicated. A website with a photo of the face behind the fake name. A Facebook page where this person who does not exist writes witticisms about getting naked. Maybe a Twitter feed where she offers followers a creative sexual position of the day, described in 140 characters or less. In short, this person who used to be just a paragraph is now much more. She has opinions. She cracks jokes. She stays up too late and needs espresso shots to get going in the morning. She's as real as anything else in the digital universe.

It's a little like suffering from multiple personality disorder, except I am acutely aware of it.

When it came time for K. T. Briggs's book jacket photos to be taken, I asked the photographer to make me look like I wrote about sex. Do your best for this very cool lady I invented who has to share a face and body with me. Please. The results were spectacular and do not resemble me in the least. I plastered them all over the K. T. Briggs website and have been known to visit there when I need a pick-me-up. K. T. Briggs lives alone on the Upper West Side of New York in a sleek, modern apartment. The kitchen gleams with stainless-steel appliances she never uses because she does not cook. She has an assortment of lovers, all handsome and successful. Her closet is stuffed with couture. She gets invited to parties. She has manicures. She never picks up anyone's laundry, and she writes saucy books. No doubt about it, K. T. Briggs is fabulous.

Of course, I might have done things a little differently if I had considered the implications. For example, the book tour. My fans are expecting K. T. Briggs, and when they get me, I can see the disappointment on their faces. I am not at all what they expected. But nobody looks like her picture on the book jacket, and readers should know that by now.

So while sharing space with K. T. Briggs can be complicated, I love her dearly. In many ways, she saved my life. When I first invented her, I was still under the cloud of heartbreak. More than anything, I wanted to be free of the misery. I wanted to create a lovely, thick bubble around myself and live there alone forever, safe from the cruelty of the outside world. Having an imaginary life, the life of K. T. Briggs, to fall back on was remarkably liberating. It got to the point where I thought everybody should have a pseudonym to hide behind when trouble showed up.

From the looks of it, Lily doesn't want an imaginary life, or at least not the one I have imagined for her. She wants her freedom. But is it my job to give her that? I'm not sure I'm brave enough to mess with the rules to that extent.

We return to the dining room to find Aidan and Jason studiously ignoring each other.

"Are we ready, my love?" Aidan says, jumping from his seat. "Do we need to hold hands like when we tried the spells before?" I can practically see his heart swell beneath his shirt. So this is great. I've got a romantic heroine who wants to be an independent single gal in New York City and I've got a romantic hero who has gone positively soft with love. What a mess.

Lily flashes me a look. Please. Help me.

"Why don't we all sit down?" I suggest.

Jason taps his watch again. "Time, Sadie," he says, as we sit.

"I understand," I say. I don't know how I'm supposed to put this. I close my eyes and imagine a blank page on my mental computer. How would I write this scene if I knew I could not delete?

"Aidan," I say. "Lily really likes you. She thinks you're strong and handsome and . . . nice. But she feels she hasn't known you long enough to commit to something like love."

I sound like a grade school counselor. Lily kicks me under the table, but I ignore her. I'm not prepared to tell Aidan she is pretty sure she's never going to love him.

In any case, I've said plenty. Aidan's face falls. His eyes grow dark. I can see him closing in on himself, shutting down. This sort of news delivered directly from the person of your desires is bad enough but from me, it is pure humiliation.

"I'm sorry," Lily whispers. But Aidan won't even look at her. He is utterly still.

"You're nothing special," he says finally. "You're just another girl in a sea of them. No big deal."

My heart aches for him. I want to hold him like I do Allison when she's hurt, pull him into my lap, wrap my arms around him, and tell him everything is going to be okay. But it's not going to be okay. In about ten minutes, Clarissa is going to march through my front door and send us all off to hell. I have made a big mistake. I have responsibilities. I have a child. Panic begins to rise in my throat. Jason puts a hand on my thigh and squeezes.

"Is our bag of tricks empty?" he asks quietly. He wants to know if I'm going to tell Aidan that Clarissa loved him in another time and in another place. But I cannot hurt Aidan any more. And I don't think it will make a difference. The ending is out of our hands.

"Yes," I say.

We sit around the dining room table, like we're holding a vigil. The air is still and hot and filled with unexpressed emotions. My wine is warm, but I drink it anyway. It does little to slow my racing heart and the feeling of strong, determined hands closing around my neck.

"Do you know what she's going to do when she gets here?" Lily asks me. "Do you think it will hurt?"

She keeps surprising me. She may cease to exist in mere minutes, but she is not melting down and she is not willing to compromise what she feels just to survive.

"I don't know," I say.

"I think everything about Clarissa hurts," Aidan says. And as the words spill from his lips, I hear the front door swing open.

"She's here," I say.

In the center hallway, beside a fresh-cut bunch of flowers in a crystal vase, stands Clarissa. Her eyes gleam at the sight of us.

"Oh good," she says, looking at Aidan. "I was worried I'd be late and miss the fireworks." She laughs at her joke.

"What do you want?" Jason asks, taking a step in front of me.

"Only what is mine," she says, pulling a flower from the water and tucking it behind her ear. In all the blackness, the red flower looks terribly lonely. "Aidan knows he accepted my deal and has now failed to deliver. It's only fair, wouldn't you say?"

I like that Jason is between Clarissa and me. It's comforting. Not that I think he has a chance in hell of defending me if she starts in chanting and waving her hands around. But still, I like it.

"You're right, you know," Aidan says flatly. He steps toward Clarissa. "Lily doesn't love me. I thought she did. I was sure. But she doesn't."

I see fear in Lily's eyes, as if she is just now realizing the steep price of freedom.

"Oh, silly boy," Clarissa says, opening her arms to Aidan. "I could have saved you the trouble. You belong to me. You always have and always will. There is nothing that can come between us."

Before stepping into her embrace, Aidan casts a glance over his shoulder at us. He gives me a smile and a wink, like I'm in on it. My insides clench with pain, and I almost double over. What is he doing? Lily is by my side. She shakes from head to toe. As Clarissa's black-clad arms wrap around Aidan, she closes her eyes and inhales his essence. She begins to chant, so quietly I cannot hear the words.

"Hold on to her," Aidan says over his shoulder. "Hold on to Lily. Hold her, Sadie, and don't let go!"

Clarissa appears not to have heard a word he has spoken. I link my arm through Lily's. Jason moves to her right and puts his arm around her shoulders. What does Aidan think he's doing? Now is not the time to throw himself on the sword. We can't let Clarissa win. But Aidan is doing only what he was destined to. Sacrificing himself for love. He's making the ultimate dramatic gesture.

The room fills with the same thick yellow light we saw earlier in the guest bedroom. Clarissa is taking Aidan back with her, and God only knows what is to become of Lily.

But this is too much. This will not do. Aidan and Lily are my responsibility, and I love them as though they are my children. I let go of Lily and take a step forward. I don't know what I'm going to do. Hit Clarissa on the head with the vase? Curse at her? Tell her to get the hell out of my book? She's too preoccupied with Aidan in her arms to notice my advance. But Jason notices.

"Stop right there," he hisses. "Don't take another step. You hold Lily. Let me."

"Forget it," I say. "This is my mess. I need to fix it."

"I'm the man," he says.

"So what?"

Clarissa continues to whisper in Aidan's ear. His eyes close, and his head falls back as if he's hypnotized.

"So those are my rules," he says. "I need to protect you."

"I'm fine," I mutter. I'm not, obviously. I'm frozen in place. I have no idea what scene comes next. If I were writing, this would be the moment I stop to make more coffee. "Shit."

"Back up," Jason demands.

"Sadie," Lily says. "Listen to him."

"No," I say. Aidan's head jerks forward. His mouth hangs open. All his masculine power is gone. He's an empty sack.

I can take a lot of criticism. I can take an editor gutting my story, because that is the deal I entered into when I signed on the dotted line. But I cannot take some unfinished character with a chip on her shoulder taking my story in a direction in which it was never meant to go. A girl has to have limits.

I rush forward, grabbing the vase.

"No," Jason yells. "Sadie, I love you, goddamn it! Stop!"

His words hit me like lightning. I stumble from the jolt of their power. But I have momentum. I fall into Aidan, clutching the back of his shirt. The aura Clarissa has spun around her is mesmerizing. It's like slipping into a warm bath up to your chin. My heart immediately calms.

But just as suddenly, the aura disappears.

"What did he say?" Clarissa asks, her face a look of pure horror. She stares at Jason.

"I said I love Sadie," Jason repeats. "I love her. I really love her. I would travel to the ends of the earth for her. And back again. I would do *anything*."

Oh, those words!

What follows is a bloodcurdling scream, high-pitched and agonizing. For a moment, I have no idea where it is coming from. Am I screaming? Lily? Did Greta discover she was missing an ingredient for the beef dish?

But the scream comes from Clarissa. She releases Aidan. She holds her hands to her ears and howls.

"What the hell?" Jason shouts above the noise. Aidan backs away from Clarissa. She starts to writhe as if suffering from a seizure, spinning and contorting right in front of us.

She is also fading. Her edges blur and melt. She looks like

everyone does to me when I take out my contact lenses. She stops screaming long enough to recognize this new state of affairs. She runs her hands up her arms. Is she still here? Her eyes focus on me. They are hot little coals, glowing red. I shudder. She is a terrifying vision.

"You take everything," Clarissa bellows. "This was supposed to be easy. Aidan was mine. He'd finally come back to me, and you had to ruin it with your magic!"

My magic? What is she talking about? She begins to spark like one of those cake toppers, little bits of light shooting off her in every direction. The air smells of char.

Jason is beside me. I lean against him. It's like a roadside car wreck, one you must slow down and look at even if you don't really want to.

In my mind, I see the box into which I put my heart all those years ago. It's dusty and shows the wear of time. Tentatively, I pick it up. It's lighter than I expected. I slip one finger under the flap that seals it shut and pry it open. Inside, the box is empty because my heart is pounding, steady and firm, in my chest.

"I love you too," I say to Jason. Love is my magic. I have to let it out, let it flow and not fear what will happen when I do. Without risk, there can be no joy. And suddenly I understand this is not about Aidan and Lily and their story. No, it's *my* story. Clarissa made the outcome of Aidan's deal dependent on me because she was sure that was the safest bet. It was almost foolproof. I would never understand the magic. I think I might faint.

"Oh my God!" Lily has jumped into Aidan's arms. He holds her tightly. They stare at the mess that is Clarissa. "What's happening?"

"The spell," Aidan shouts above the noise. "She bet her life she would win."

I close my eyes, the image of the witch burning in my hallway seared on my eyelids. All of a sudden, there's a loud roar from behind me. Greta, holding our industrial-size fire extinguisher, marches down the hallway.

"This is an old house, Sadie," she says. "We need to be careful." With that, she aims the nozzle at Clarissa and lets loose.

Chapter 34

We all stand around the pile of black dust. No one says a word. Greta has returned to the kitchen, muttering about carelessness and old wood.

"Is she gone?" Lily asks tentatively. Jason sticks a toe into the dust.

"I think so," he says. I have yet to take a really close look at his face. Is it going to register pure disbelief? And if it does, what does that mean for us? He holds my hand. I squeeze. He squeezes back. I take that as a good sign, at least for now.

"I thought I was going to be dead," Lily says. "I was prepared to be dead. But I'm not dead. Am I?"

I shake my head. No. They are not dead. But they are still here. Aidan, who has not said a word, finally speaks up.

"We've got a problem," he says.

"Yes," I say. "We've got a lot of problems, but at least we can check 'witch' off the list, right?"

"No, Sadie," he says. "We're got a real problem." He holds up his hand, fingers spread, palm facing me. And I can almost see right through him. He's fading. As is Lily beside him.

"No, no, no, no!" I shriek. "This isn't fair."

For the first time in two days, I'm furious.

"None of this was supposed to happen," I yell. "*Stolen Secrets* was about these two falling in love! There were no witches or spells or magic or random disappearances to other realities!"

I feel betrayed, but by whom I cannot say.

"So make it that," Jason says, with some urgency. "Do it. Write it. Now."

Write it now. Make it go the way I'd intended. Make everyone happy. Give it a "happily ever after." I grab Jason by the shoulders and give him a shake.

"Get my laptop and meet me upstairs," I say. "Aidan and Lily, don't disappear. Not yet. Please."

I sprint to my office and sweep everything off my desk. I pull up my chair. I take a few deep breaths. I look out the window into the darkness. Jason arrives, panting, and drops my laptop in front of me. The machine is cold and dead. I fumble in the top desk drawer for the power cord and plug it in.

For a minute, I think nothing is going to happen. But then it whirs to life and the happy little apple comes dancing into view. I want to kiss it. Oh, I've missed you these past two days! I have so much to tell you.

I click on the icon for the *Stolen Secrets* manuscript. It pops up. The word count stands at exactly where I left it when I went to bed two nights ago. There is nothing left of Clarissa on the pages.

I've done some stupid things in my life. A lot of things, actually, but I've never been fool enough to try and bang out an entire novel in one sitting. But my characters are fading away before my very eyes, and if I don't get them on the page, if I can't preserve them there, I might lose them forever. And there is a very real pain in losing characters you love.

"What do you need, Sadie?" Jason asks as I touch my fingers to the keyboard.

"Just stay with me, okay?" Be my muse.

"Of course," he says.

"But you can't talk," I say. "That's distracting."

He laughs, pulling an advance copy of my latest novel, due to hit the shelves in four weeks, from a cardboard delivery box. He lies back on the couch and begins to read, just as if he's done this a thousand times before. I begin to type.

Aidan Hathaway sat on the broad black leather sofa with his feet up. They had decided to meet here in his office, on neutral ground, because it might make things easier. He reminded himself that he already knew what Lily was coming here to say. He felt it too. It was undeniable.

They tried, but in the end, physical lust was not

enough. They did not love each other, and that was the cold, hard truth. But it was okay because it went both ways. No one would end up brokenhearted if they both accepted defeat.

It had started when Aidan was out with his best childhood friend, Erin. Erin was bright and sassy, short and round and smarter than almost anyone Aidan had ever met. They had known each other since grade school, and their friendship had blossomed in recent years as Aidan found himself more and more isolated from regular people. Erin worked as a DA for the city of New York, and the stories she brought him were little gifts, full of drama and madness. He could listen to her for hours. All night long, in fact, and often did.

Which was part of the problem with Lily. When he was with Lily, he found he missed Erin. At first he dismissed it as a feeling totally appropriate for a good and reliable friend, but after a while even he had to examine it more closely.

He thought he might love Erin. He thought he might be in love with his best friend after all.

Aidan was lost in this thought when Lily knocked gently on his office door. His secretary was long gone, the hum of the building the only sound.

"Come in," he said.

Lily gave him a small smile. He could never see her without losing his breath, she was that beautiful. Today, her strawberry-blond curls hung loose down past her shoulders, and her bright purple dress hugged her curves as he often had these last months. He would miss being in bed with her, running his hands over her soft, pale skin, hearing her moans of pleasure. But it wasn't enough, and they both knew it. In a way, he was proud of her for taking the initiative, as he had been unable to do.

"You look tired," she said, sitting beside him on the couch and running her fingers down his rough cheek.

"Long day," he said. "Nonsense in China."

"Of course," she said. "But if anyone can handle it, it's you."

"Thanks, Lily." He draped an arm across her shoulders.

"You know why I'm here." It wasn't a question.

He nodded.

"We tried," she continued. "We did. And we've had fun, and I know that ex-lovers can't often succeed as friends, but I feel differently about us. I think we can if we try. Can we try, Aidan?"

"Oh, Lily," he said. He drew her in and kissed her. It was a long, sweet kiss, and it told her everything he could not. He did love her. She would always be in his life. They would both make it. Just not together.

"Yes," he said, finally pulling away. "We can try." He felt her relax in his arms. He knew through his sources that she didn't have anyone else, but that wouldn't last. A woman as beautiful as Lily was only alone by choice.

In the end, they wanted different things. He wanted someone who understood him to the point where he did not need to explain himself. He wanted a woman who loved him for who he was, not for what he could offer. He wanted Erin.

"She's here, you know," Lily said, sliding away from him. Was she reading his mind?

"Who?" Aidan asked.

"You know," she said with a coy smile. "And it's okay. She loves you, really loves you. She would do anything for you. And I suspect you feel the same way. Right?"

Aidan gave her an almost imperceptible nod. His heart raced. Was all of this really happening? He was supposed to get on a plane to Hong Kong tomorrow. Could he do that when his life was so unsettled?

"And I told her to pack a bag," Lily said. She stood now and smoothed invisible wrinkles from her dress. She removed one stiletto heel, wiggled her toes, and put it back on. She picked up her leather briefcase, the one he had given her in better times, and smiled. It was not a smile of defeat. It was warm and open, and it gave him permission to be happy with someone else, to be happy with Erin.

"Thank you, Lily," he said, rising from the couch.

"Good-bye, Aidan," she said. Without looking back she strode through the open office door. The last thing Aidan would ever see of Lily Dell was that stiletto heel, rounding a corner and vanishing.

 Happily Ever After

Erin once said love will find a way in. It may be tricky
and it may surprise you, but it will find a way.

And for now, he had to agree that she was right.

I close the laptop. I take a deep breath. I have broken all the
rules.

Chapter 35

It is 6:00 A.M. The sun is just beginning to show itself on the horizon. My desk is littered with small ceramic espresso cups, delivered every hour on the hour by Greta. My hands shake, and I'm sure if I look in the mirror my eyes will resemble pinwheels. But I did it. I gave them an ending.

Jason snores on the couch, his head at an awkward angle. Earlier, I told him to go to bed, but he refused.

"I'm staying right here," he said. If I started to disappear, he was not going to miss the chance to grab me.

It's cold now, the heat wave broken. I pull a wool wrap around my shoulders and quietly push back from my desk. My body aches from sitting in the same position for hours on end. I pop and crack as I stretch toward the ceiling. On tiptoe, I pad down the hallway to the guest room, where Aidan and Lily retired. I told them I did not know what would happen but I would use some of the best magic I have, my love of words. I nudge open the closed door. The room is bathed in the soft light of morning, the kind that can make the most drab scene beautiful.

On the bed lies Lily, her red hair fanned out against the white pillowcase. She lies on her side, with her two hands tucked beneath her cheek. She looks like an angel, peaceful and quiet.

She is also fully formed. There are no blurry spots or ragged edges. And Aidan, quite simply, is gone. The only evidence that he was ever here is the slight head-shaped indent on the pillow beside Lily.

I will never know if she watched him fade or what they said to each other as their bond was severed forever. Maybe they didn't say anything. Maybe they were sleeping and the whole thing felt like a dream.

Greta appears silently at my shoulder, a faint smile on her lips.

"Will this be her room?" Greta whispers.

"For now," I say.

Greta rests a hand on my shoulder. Her touch startles me. "She reminds me of you when we first met," she says. "Things happen, but you don't stop. You don't go around. You go through the hard stuff. We can all learn from that."

My eyes well up. I'm exhausted and overwhelmed but more calm than I've been in years. Greta disappears as quietly as she came.

Love comes in. It comes in Allison and Roger and Jason and

Aidan and Lily. It comes in Greta and my agent, Liz, and Ellen, my rule-obsessed fan. It comes in my readers and the friends who meet me for coffee. It comes in the moms on the quad. It comes in the pages I'm so lucky to write when I'm alone. Love is all around me, but until now, I did not recognize it as the only glue necessary to bind the pieces of me together. It is what makes me whole.

Love is tricky, and it has certainly surprised me, but it has found a way in.

Chapter 36

Twelve Weeks Later

sit at my desk and stare into space. The fragrance of fresh-cut grass floats through my window and makes my nose tickle. Open on the screen of my brand-new laptop is an e-mail from Ellen. She likes my latest book. She thinks I might finally be getting it.

Thanks for sticking with me, I write back. I very much appreciate it.

I do not tell her that once she reads *Stolen Secrets* she will go right back to hating me. But that's okay. I like it. It might be my favorite book so far.

Allison sits on the small sofa, reading the latest hot teenage vampire bestseller. She chews her fingernails and twirls her hair in a way that reminds me of Aidan Hathaway. But she's here in my office with me by choice, so I don't mention the correlation between hair twirling and bald spots. I enjoy her presence. From downstairs comes a racket of pots and pans being slammed around.

"Mom, when are they going to stop doing that?" Allison asks.

"Probably never," I say. "Greta's hard-core, honey."

Upon learning she would be staying, Lily jumped into this reality with determination. She even went so far as to ask Greta to teach her how to cook. Not scrambled eggs and toast, mind you, but real food. Greta, thrilled to have an enthusiastic protégée, now has Lily braising short ribs for dinner. It's a tempestuous relationship, at least on Greta's side. She is not the world's most patient teacher, especially if there is a chance her student is going to injure a perfectly innocent hunk of meat. Lily takes the abuse with good humor. She is easy to have around. And really, if I'd started making babies sometime before my late thirties, I could have had a daughter the same age as Lily, so it isn't totally strange to have her living under my roof. We are a house of women.

Soon Jason will arrive. He's always invited when Greta and Lily have spent the day in the kitchen. He'll show up with his tie undone and his sleeves rolled up. He'll kiss me hard when he thinks no one is looking.

We go on dates now, just the two of us. It's nice to hold hands in a dark movie theater or share a small table tucked away in the back corner of a restaurant. We talk on the

phone every day. If I hear something funny, I call and tell him. I had forgotten about all the little things in a relationship that make it sweet. We don't struggle to figure out what is going to happen tomorrow, because tomorrow will happen regardless.

And often, after Allison has gone to bed and I've hit a word count I can live with, Jason will sneak in our back door and spend the night with me. But no matter what else is going on, we try never to miss a Friday morning, because only a fool would vote to cancel a really good thing on purpose.

We have yet to discuss the events of three months earlier. I refer to it as "the heat wave," and it's common knowledge everyone goes a little insane during a heat wave. Jason always smiles when it comes up, but sometimes I wonder if any of it really happened. Maybe I just fell over in my desk chair and hit my head on the bookcase or something. Or it was in my dreams? But then I see Lily, and that line between reality and fantasy blurs. I'm bungee-jumping on the shoelace. It could all be fine, but you never know.

My cell phone rings.

"Hello?"

"It's Liz, honey," my agent says. "How are you? Haven't heard from you in at least a week. What're you working on?"

I don't want to tell, but I find it impossible to lie to Liz.

"Paranormal," I say quietly. Maybe she won't hear me.

"You did *not* just say paranormal, Sadie."

"I did," I say. "Remember the one with the witches? Clarissa and Evangeline?"

"No," she says, a little hot, "because you never showed it to me. You told me it was shit and should never see the light of day. Why now?"

Because I denied Clarissa her own story, so she pushed her way into another one. She wanted closure. Don't we all? And by my calculations, if it happened once, it can happen again. Who's to say if, left to her own devices, Evangeline won't pop up next, seeking revenge for Clarissa? I can't have that happen. It would be a mess.

Really I'm hedging my bets. If I give them their own book, perhaps they will leave me alone. Besides, now I think I know how it's going to end. I'm going to give them a happily ever after. It will be shocking.

"I'm ready for it," I say.

"Fine, honey," Liz says. "You tinker around all you want if it makes you happy."

I wouldn't say it makes me happy. Despite recent events, I'm still not a great paranormal writer. But I owe my witch. I've been Xanax free for three months now. I feel remarkably calm. I have not even been biting my nails, waiting for feedback from my publisher on *Stolen Secrets*. It's downright strange, and without Clarissa, I'm not sure any of it would have happened.

"Maybe," I say, "in a way."

"Well, I'm glad, but that's not the reason I called," Liz says. "Let's talk about *Stolen Secrets*."

They hated it.

"They loved it! It wasn't like your usual fare, but it appears to have struck a nerve. They want a sequel. Can you do that for me, honey? I said you'd need at least three months."

Did she just say sequel?

Dear me.

Acknowledgments

As always, thank you to my agent, Leigh Feldman. Without Leigh, nothing happens and I'm grateful to her every day. Plus, she's fun, and that's important. Next, a big thank you to my editor, Heather Lazare, for carefully crafting this book into what it was meant to be and for getting it to the finish line before Mother Nature interrupted. I think this is what they mean when they say "team effort."

I know I've said this before but I owe everything to my family. So thank you to my kids for being funny and curious and good little souls. In my son, I have finally met a reader as voracious as myself. It warms my heart and also empties my bank account. All proceeds from *Happily Ever After* will be spent feeding him books. And of course, thank you to Mike, for still thinking having an author wife is cool and for never once rolling his eyes when I say "I have the *greatest* idea!" Also, a big shout-out to my in-laws, Bob and Becky McMullen, for picking up what is sometimes a whole lot of slack.

Finally, and most importantly, this is for my readers. I'm grateful to each and every one of you, and if I can help you escape reality for just a little while, I will consider this effort a success. Happy reading.

Elizabeth Maxwell
Davis, California
April 17, 2013

Happily

Ever After

This reading group guide for *Happily Ever After* includes an introduction, discussion questions, a conversation with the author, and ideas for enhancing your book club. The suggested questions are intended to help your reading group find new and interesting angles and topics for your discussion. We hope these ideas will enrich your conversation and increase your enjoyment of the book.

Sadie Fuller is a fairly typical forty-six-year-old divorced mom—a little overweight, unlucky in love, and stuck in the suburbs with no shortage of responsibilities. But Sadie is not like the other soccer moms on her block: while her daughter is at school, Sadie writes erotic fiction, creating steamy fantasies starring beautiful, scantily clad characters who have exactly nothing to do with her real life. Then, an unexpected plot twist causes a break with reality, and Sadie finds herself face-to-face with what appears to be her latest romantic hero in the baby products aisle at the local Target. She has no idea how he got there—or how to get him safely back into the pages of her book. But she's determined to give him a "happily ever after," and perhaps create one for herself this time, too.

For Discussion

1. *Happily Ever After* opens with the definition of the term "midlife crisis." How does this set the tone for the story? How well do you think this definition applies to what Sadie goes through?

2. On page 41, Sadie is worried her relationship with Jason may be doomed if he's not a reader. She declares, "A man who reads is profoundly sexy. A man who does not is just some guy." Do you agree? What qualities or characteristics would you consider deal breakers?

3. Throughout the story, the dichotomy between city and country life often comes up. Sadie seems to have love/hate relationships with both settings, though she chose suburban life for her daughter's sake. What is your preference? How does your experience of either the city or the country compare to Sadie's?

4. Even though Lily and Aidan were products of Sadie's imagination, they end up taking on lives of their own—in more ways than one! How do they turn out to be different than

Sadie had intended? What do you think they end up teaching Sadie about herself by not following her plans?

5. At separate points in the story, Sadie and Jason both seem to readily accept the magical truth of what is actually happening as it's presented to them. Were you surprised that they weren't more incredulous? Would you have been so easily convinced?

6. Sadie takes on many different roles in life—roles that she's often trying to keep distinctly separate from one another. Discuss the many titles she adopts and how successfully she juggles them.

7. For a while, both before she got pregnant and after her divorce, Sadie was tempted to give up on her happy ending. Have you ever felt ready to throw in the towel? Do you think Sadie ever really gave up?

8. Compare Sadie's relationship with Jason to the types of relationships she writes about in her books. Does their story follow the rules of a good book—according to Ellen or according to you?

9. So many of the characters in this book are faced with heartache at one point or another. Discuss how they each seem to deal with it and what you think that says about them. How

does heartache help bring any of them together or move the story along?

10. *Happily Ever After* features a witch, spells, and alternate realities. What effect does it have on your belief—or suspension of disbelief—in the story?

11. Sadie shows a lot of care for her characters when trying to break Clarissa's spells. Why do you think she is willing to go through so much trouble and even endanger herself to try to save them? Would you have done the same?

12. On page 303, Sadie says, "sometimes I wonder if any of it really happened . . . But then I see Lily, and that line between reality and fantasy blurs." What do you make of Lily's decision to stay with Sadie? How would it have changed the story if she hadn't stayed? Would you have believed it had all really happened?

13. Discuss the endings for each of the main characters. Do they all get a "happily ever after"? Do you wish it had ended differently for any of them?

A Conversation with Elizabeth Maxwell

Congratulations on your first novel! Have you always wanted to be an author? What led you down this path?

Yes! But it always felt like a bit of a fantasy, the sort of thing you say when someone asks you what you want to be when you grow up. To make it real, I had to break it down into small chunks, sentence by sentence, page by page. I tried never to think about the endgame, as in, "What am I going to do with this story when I'm done?" because that's paralyzing. "Focus on the writing" became my daily mantra.

What inspired the unique story of *Happily Ever After*? How did the plot and the characters evolve?

The story evolved a few different ways. First, I read about an erotic fiction author who lives in the southern United States and doesn't tell anyone what she does for a living. I love the idea that things are seldom what they seem so this was right up my alley. I could not stop imagining the consequences of such a secret on a person's day-to-day life.

Second, I was with my literary agent and we were talking about the movie *Enchanted* and how fun it is to mash genres together. That got me thinking of a framework for a story about a closet erotic fiction author who's coming a little un-glued.

How do you compare with Sadie as a writer? Do you have similar habits, work ethics, rules?

Sadie is a genre writer and therefore has a greater appreci-ation of genre rules than I do. She knows if she's writing erotica it better go a certain way or she's going to hear about it from her fans. I think a lot less about the container my story needs to fit into and much more about what I want to tell. But we both take incredibly sloppy notes!

Aside from having the same occupation, do you relate to Sadie in any other ways?

It was incredibly satisfying to write about a fortysomething woman, which I am. It's amazing how little play characters of this age get in fiction today. It's almost as if women in fic-tion reach age thirty-five and simply vanish. It was also fun to juxtapose the very real trials of Sadie's life and age with the fantasy elements of the novel. I wanted it to be fun but also look at how complicated love and relationships can be.

Although you currently live in California, you chose to set this novel in and around the New York City area. Have you ever lived in New York or spent significant time there? Why did you choose it for your setting?

I love New York! I grew up there and even though I've lived out west for almost fifteen years now, I will always be a New Yorker at heart. I knew immediately when I began to work on *Happily* that the suburbs surrounding New York City set the perfect tone for Sadie's conflict.

Happily Ever After has elements of women's fiction, erotica, and fantasy all wrapped up together. What was the most fun to write? What was the most challenging?

My hat is off to erotica writers and paranormal writers! It's incredibly hard to do this well—you have to be mindful of not crossing the line that makes a reader abandon your book because it feels too ridiculous. I fell over that line many times, but thankfully there are editors and drafts (many, many of them)!

What are your favorite kinds of books to read for fun? Is there a particular author or book that inspired your writing style? Are there any other genres you'd still like to tackle?

I'll read anything as long as it grabs me. Authors I love include Susan Isaacs, Stephen King, Janet Evanovich, Alexandra Fuller, Alice Hoffman, Kate Atkinson, Hilary Mantel, Curtis Sittenfeld, Diane Setterfield, Katherine Neville, and early Harlan Coben.

I'd love to write a murder mystery—I have a really great

ending; it's just the other three hundred pages I'm struggling with.

Do you have a favorite character? Did they always behave as you intended or were you ever thrown for a loop by your own creations, just as Sadie was?

I'm a terrible outliner, so sometimes my characters take off in directions I never saw coming. On a good day, it works out and by the time I hit Save I understand why they did what they did. On a bad day, I end up deleting a full day's work because none of it makes any sense. The hope is that there are ultimately more good days than bad.

You wrote on page 130, "Backstory is a funny thing. It can make its way to paper or stay tucked away in a writer's head." Did you have any other backstory developed for these characters that never made its way to paper?

Tons! There are so many bits and pieces that ultimately do not make it to the page because of story or space constraints or just a lack of relevancy. For instance, I know what Sadie likes for lunch, but there are more important details the reader needs to know about her when it comes to moving the story forward. And every detail has to count.

But I keep it all because I never know when I might revisit these characters or use some of their backstory details for another character in another novel.

What message do you hope readers will take away from *Happily Ever After*?

The world is a strange and mysterious place. Magic is all around us in our everyday lives, it just depends on how you look at things.

Are you working on a new novel? Would you ever consider writing a sequel?

Yes and yes. Right now, I'm working on a novel; I'm again concerned with how things are not always as they appear. This work is a little bit darker, however, and there are no witches.

As for sequels, every author wants to do a sequel because it means the original stirred something in readers, and that's all I really want—for readers to walk away having enjoyed the ride.

Enhance Your Book Club

1. Sadie has created a whole biography for K.T. Briggs. If you had to come up with a pen name, what would it be? What kind of bio would you write for your alter ego's book cover? Take a stab at it!

2. Sadie's fan Ellen certainly had her ideas about what made for a good romance novel. Do you have any rules for what you think is a good book? Maybe you're a sucker for happy endings, or you love an unexpected plot twist. Try coming up with a few rules of your own and share them when you discuss *Happily Ever After*. Do they apply to this book?

3. According to Sadie, Roger's yoga studio is always suffering for one reason or another. Find a local yoga studio to support with your book club and make it a group trip!

Learn more about Elizabeth Maxwell, read her blog, and find out how to follow her on Twitter by visiting ElizabethMaxwell Author.com.